Reckoning

She
she
asi
mo

in
tha

the
Vil
Di
c
p
t
f
n

Read all of **the fallen** titles:

The Fallen

Leviathan

Aerie

Reckoning

Available from Simon Pulse

the fallen

Book Four

reckoning

Thomas E. Sniegoski

Simon Pulse

NEW YORK   LONDON   TORONTO   SYDNEY

This book is a work of fiction. Any references to historical events,
real people, or real locales are used fictitiously. Other names, characters,
places, and incidents are the product of the author's imagination, and any
resemblance to actual events or locales or persons, living or dead,
is entirely coincidental.

First Simon Pulse edition March 2004

Copyright © 2004 by Thomas E. Sniegoski

SIMON PULSE
An imprint of Simon & Schuster
Children's Publishing Division
1230 Avenue of the Americas
New York, NY 10020

Designed by Sammy Yuen Jr.
The text of this book was set in 11 point Palatino.

Printed in the United States of America
2   4   6   8   10   9   7   5   3   1

Library of Congress Control Number 2003108404

ISBN 0-689-85308-4

*In loving memory of Carol A. Giordano. I'm
sure she has God laughing.*

To LeeAnne for inspiring me with her love, and
to Mulder for always making me smile.

Great gobs of gooey thanks to my creepy little
brother, Christopher Golden, and to the best
dang editor a cowpoke could have, Lisa Clancy.

And thanks prepared in a delicious red wine
sauce must be served to: Mom & Dad; Eric "The
Goon" Powell; Dave "Fancy Britches" Kraus;
David Carroll; Dr. Kris; Tom & Lori Stanley and
their wonder twins; Paul Griffin; Tim Cole and
the usual cast of crazies; Jon & Flo; Bob & Pat;
Don Kramer; Pete Donaldson; Ken Curtis; Joan
Reilly; Allie Costa; and Debra and Michael
Sundin at the Hearts & Stars Bookshop.

It's been a great ride. Thank you, and good
night.

reckoning

prologue

Maybe it's time to move on, the Malakim Peliel considered as he perched atop Mount Kilimanjaro, nineteen thousand feet above the arid African plains of Tanzania.

The angelic being could count on one hand the number of times he'd had this thought in his two-millennia stay upon the dormant volcanic mountain. But always something distracted him from these musings. The coming of so-called civilization as villages turned to cities, seeming to grow up from the earth to replace the primordial jungles. The vast springtime migrations of wildebeests, zebras, antelopes, gazelles, and lions as they made their way across the Serengeti's southern plains to greener pastures in nearby Kenya. *There is so much to see here*, he reminded himself. *So much to feel, to hear, to smell.* And wasn't that his purpose—the purpose of being Malakim? He and his brethren around the globe acted as God's senses, enabling the Supreme Being to experience the wonders of the world He created.

However, today was different. Something in the thin, frigid air of Kilimanjaro was telling him—warning him—that perhaps it would be wise to seek another roost.

Slowly, Peliel flexed millennial stiffness from his wings. The collected layers of dirt and ice that had clung to his stationary form over the thousands of years fell away to reveal a creature of Heaven in what had appeared to be just another natural formation dappling the frozen landscape.

"There you are," said a voice even colder than the winds blowing across the mountaintop.

The Malakim gracefully turned, finding himself in the presence of another of God's heavenly children. This one was dressed in human garb, accompanied by twenty of his ilk, and seemed to be the source of Peliel's unease. "What host are you?" Peliel asked, casually brushing dirt from his intricate armor.

"I am Verchiel," the intruder answered, bowing slightly, "of the heavenly host Powers."

Peliel studied the beings before him, taking note of the multitude of angry scars that adorned the exposed flesh of their bodies. This angelic army had been in battle against a foe that also wielded the power of the divine; there was no other way to explain the marks of conflict they carried. *What has transpired while my attentions were elsewhere?* the Malakim wondered.

"Ah yes, the hunters of the fallen," Peliel commented aloud, the wind howling about him as if in warning. "You have been searching for me, Verchiel of the Powers?" To his own ears, his voice was gruff from millenia of non-use, like the grinding of tectonic plates within the earth's crust. "And why would that be?"

It pleased him to speak again, and his mind wandered back to the last time he had used his voice to communicate. Many centuries past, a jungle cat, a leopard, had inexplicably climbed close to the western summit of the great mountain. Curious of the creature's intent, Peliel had appeared before the animal. It was dying, the frigid climate of Kilimanjaro's winter season sapping the warmth from its lithe, spotted body, and in the language of its species, the Malakim had asked it why it had come to such an inhospitable place. As it lay down in the snow to die, the leopard had responded that it had been drawn up the mountain, tempted by the desire to bear witness to something greater than itself—lured by the powerful emanations of the Malakim. Peliel smiled, wondering if this was the reason these Powers had come, drawn by a sense of his omnipotence.

"I am in need of something you have in your possession," Verchiel interrupted the Malakim's musings.

Peliel chuckled, amused by this angel's arrogance. "And what could I have that would possibly interest you, little messenger?"

"You and the others of your kind are direct conduits to God," Verchiel explained. "Extensions of His holy power—receptacles for His wisdom and knowledge."

Peliel crossed his arms across his broad chest, silently urging the angel to continue with a nod of his head.

"I require information concerning the deconstruction of God's Word . . . and I shall have it no matter the cost," Verchiel proclaimed.

Peliel's ire was rankled by the presumption. *How dare this angel think himself worthy to make demands of a Malakim?* "Tread carefully, Verchiel," the Malakim growled, "for it is within my might to see you punished for your conceit." He unfurled his great wings of gunmetal gray, the very air around him crackling with restrained supernatural energies.

"I'm sorry to say there is little you can subject me to, holy Malakim, that is any worse than what I have already endured," Verchiel replied, a vicious sneer appearing upon his pale, burn-mottled features. "Give me what I ask for and I shall leave you to your observation of this . . . *fascinating* continent." Malice dripped from his disrespectful words as he chanced a casual glance over the African horizon.

There is a dangerous hate in this one, the

Malakim observed, and again wondered what could have transpired while his attentions were focused elsewhere. He had no choice but to put this imperious angel, and those who followed him, in their respective places. This reckless arrogance could not be allowed to continue unchecked.

"Insolent pup!" Peliel bellowed, his voice rumbling across the mountain like the roar of an avalanche. He reached up into the icy blue sky to draw from the heavens a weapon of crackling energy, a sword of divine might. And he slammed his weapon down upon the mountaintop. The ground heaved and split where it was struck, a fissure in Kilimanjaro's rocky flesh zigzagging haphazardly toward the Powers angels as the ground beneath their feet shook.

"Rail all you like, keeper of His Word," Verchiel said, taking flight, his powerful wings lifting him from the tremulous earth. "It will change nothing." And then he raised his hand and brought it down in a silent command to those who served him.

The angels of the Powers host surged toward the Malakim, screams of violence pouring from their open maws, weapons of flame materializing in their grasps.

Peliel responded in kind, his own weapon forged from the might of the storm, incinerating the first of the attacking heavenly warriors. They were no match for him, but still they came, one after another, unto their deaths. As the last of them cried out in failure and the ashes of their bodies drifted across the frozen mountaintop, Peliel turned to face their master.

Verchiel stood unmoving, his hands clasped behind his back. There was not the slightest hint of remorse for the fate of those who obeyed his command.

"You knew that they hadn't a chance against me," the Malakim seethed, the lightning sword humming and flashing in his grip, eager to strike again.

The leader of the army so callously sent to their fates nodded in agreement.

"But still you ordered them to attack. Why? Is it your wish to die, Verchiel of the Powers host? Do you attempt to save face by being vanquished by one greater than you?"

The angel smiled, and in that instant Peliel of the Malakim was certain that the disease of madness had indeed infected this creature of Heaven. It was a smile that told him the angel was beyond caring, beyond fear of reprisal. And for the briefest of instants, the emissary of God feared the lowly messenger.

"What has happened to make you this way?" Peliel asked.

Verchiel's body grew straight and rigid. "I am what He has made me," the Powers leader growled. "The deaths of those in my charge have served a purpose." His eyes of solid black twinkled with the taint of insanity and he opened his wings as if to punctuate his mad statement. "A distraction was required."

Peliel sensed the presence of the Archons before their attack upon him, attuned as he was to the delicate thrum of angelic magicks—magicks that were taught by the Malakim. He turned to face the threat as a doorway into a place that reeked of death and decay closed behind them. There were only five Archons when there should have been seven, another sign that things were amiss. The Malakim began to ask his students what had befallen the world of God's man while he was preoccupied, but the words did not have a chance to leave his mouth.

Peliel knew the spells that flowed from their mouths, powerful magicks meant to immobilize prey of great strength, and he was preparing to counter their attack when he was viciously struck from behind. The ferocious heat of Verchiel's sword had melted through the metal of his armor and punctured the angelic flesh beneath. The Malakim whirled to confront the source of this latest affront as the last words of the Powers commander became frighteningly obvious.

"A distraction was required."

Verchiel had already leaped away and Peliel felt the spells of the Archons take hold. It was too late. He had missed his opportunity to fight back. The magick entered his body, worming its way beneath his flesh, into his muscles and bones, freezing him solid like the cold, rugged terrain on which he had dwelled these last two thousand years. His students had learned well the might of angel sorcery, and they encircled his immobilized form, gently lowering him to the icy ground as the winds swirled feverishly around them.

Peliel could feel nothing but was fully aware of all that transpired about him. Four of the Archons loomed above, muttering the incantations that kept him incapacitated. From inside his robes, the fifth of the magick users—whose eyes, Peliel noticed, had been removed from his skull—produced a tool, a knife that shimmered and glowed seductively. Its blade was curved and serrated, and the Malakim was certain that its bite would be fierce indeed.

The blind Archon plunged the blade down into Peliel's forehead with such force that his skull split wide. The world began to grow dim, and as the veil of unconsciousness drifted across his eyes, Peliel saw that Verchiel had taken his place beside his purveyors of angel magick.

"Do you see it?" he was asking over the droning repetition of the Archons' spell, a breathless impatience in his voice.

"It is there," said the magick user with a tilt of his hooded head, the vacant caverns of his eye sockets filled with swirling pools of bottomless darkness.

"Then get it for me," Verchiel demanded with a fervent hiss.

And with trembling fingers, the blind Archon reached inside the Malakim's skull to take the prize his master so desperately sought.

chapter one

Vilma Santiago pressed the phone to her ear, listening to the sounds of sadness and disappointment. She hated lying to her aunt and uncle—hated how it made her feel like a silly little girl—but the alternative was something that she herself had barely begun to comprehend, never mind her guardians.

No, I didn't really run away from home to hook up with a boy I barely knew, but was convinced that I'd fallen in love with, she wanted to tell them. *Nope, not at all. In fact I was kidnapped by real live angels as bait to lure Aaron—you know, that boy that I'm in love with—into a trap. The bad angels wanted to kill Aaron before some kind of ancient prophecy that he was supposed to represent came true. You see, Aaron is a Nephilim, the child of a human mother and an angel—and guess what, so am I. Isn't that awesome?*

She heard her aunt's voice suddenly asking if she was still there, and Vilma promptly pushed aside the truth in favor of the lies. At the moment, lies were far less trouble.

"I'm here," she said, trying to keep the tone in her voice cheerful and upbeat. "Sorry about that, I think we might have a bad connection."

The woman's questions droned on and on, the same questions that she had asked during Vilma's first call a week ago. Was she in trouble? Did she have a place to stay? When was she coming home? Vilma gazed through the glass partition in the back of the phone booth at the traffic whizzing past her on the highway across from the roadside stop. She wanted nothing more than to be in one of those cars, speeding away from her life—running from what she had learned about herself. But she knew that was impossible, because no matter how far she drove or how fast she ran, she could never escape what she truly was.

Nephilim. The word continued to haunt her. She had read about these offspring of angels and humans in the numerous books about heavenly beings she had enjoyed reading over the years, but she had never imagined that the knowledge she had gleaned would in any way, shape, or form pertain to her. It was just all so crazy.

"Are you sure you're all right?" her aunt asked yet again, and Vilma paused before allowing the lie to flow from her mouth.

The thing that made her a Nephilim—what Aaron described as an angelic essence—had awakened at the strike of midnight on her eighteenth birthday. With each passing day she could feel it growing stronger. And it scared her.

"I'm fine," she said into the phone. "I told you, I just need a little more time to figure out what I want to do with my life. As soon as I do, I'll come home. I promise."

Is that really a lie? she wondered, barely hearing her uncle's hundredth offer to come and get her wherever she was, any time of the day or night. All she had to do was call, let him know where to find her, and he would be there for her. *Will I ever be able to return to Lynn, Massachusetts—especially being the way I am now?*

Vilma felt the power stir inside her and offhandedly wondered if it was similar to the feelings women experienced when pregnant. She seriously doubted that having a baby growing inside her could ever scare her as much this. Besides, if she were having a child it would be because it was wanted. Vilma didn't want this angelic power, and sometimes she suspected that the thing inside her knew it. It was unpredictable, and she never knew when the essence would awaken and cause a fuss. She tried with all her might to keep it under control, but it was like trying to hold back a sneeze—except a sneeze didn't have the power of Heaven behind it. Every day it seemed just a little bit stronger than the day before, and Vilma worried that there would come a time when the force would be stronger than her.

Suddenly she didn't want to be on the phone anymore, just in case the power of the Nephilim decided to assert itself. Most of the time it was downright painful, and she didn't want to give her aunt and uncle any reason to be more concerned for her than they already were.

Vilma told them that she had to go and that she would call them again in a couple of days. She told them that she loved them and her niece and nephew very much, reminded them not to worry, and assured them that she would be back home soon.

And then, as the connection was broken, the power of angels thrummed through her body like the bass from a car stereo cranked to maximum, and Vilma wondered if this would be the time.

The time that she could not hold it back.

Aaron Corbet couldn't pull his eyes from the entrance to the diner across the parking lot. The elderly, families, and truck drivers—people of all shapes and sizes, heading in for breakfast and coming out satisfied. It was all so boring—so mundane.

What he wouldn't give for boring and mundane in his own life.

"*What do you think that big fat guy with the*

bald head ate?" his Labrador retriever and best friend, Gabriel, asked from his side. *"I think he just burped; I can smell sausage. I love sausage, don't you, Aaron?"*

The young man didn't answer, still caught up in the flow of normal. For just a brief moment he wanted to remember what it was like to be them—the people coming and going from the diner, oblivious to the beings from Heaven, angels, who walked among them.

"Are you thinking about sausage, Aaron?" Gabriel suddenly asked him, chasing away his brief fantasy. *"Or maybe pancakes. What I wouldn't give for some of those. Are you sure we can't go in and have something to eat? I'm very hungry."*

"No, we can't," Aaron responded, feeling again the weight of the new responsibilities he had to bear. He had come to accept them, but that did not make them any easier to carry.

The fallen angels that had fled to Earth after the war in Heaven believed in an ancient prophecy, a revelation that an offspring of a mortal woman and angel would be born into the world of man. This amalgam of God's greatest creations, this Nephilim, would be special—different from others of its ilk—and would bring with it a way in which those who had fallen from grace could be forgiven their sins and reunited with their Holy Father in Heaven. Aaron Corbet was this Nephilim—the savior—whether he liked it or not.

A family exited the restaurant—mother, father, and little boy probably about seven years old. The boy held tightly to the string of a Sponge Bob balloon, and at that moment looked to be the happiest kid in the world. Aaron watched them cross the parking lot to their car and couldn't help but think of the family that had been lost to him, violently torn away as a result of his angelic destiny.

After spending the first years of his life shuffled from one foster family to another, he was finally placed with the Stanleys, a truly loving couple, and their young, autistic son. They had accepted him as one of their own, and became the only family Aaron ever really knew. But they were all gone now, murdered by a host of angels—the Powers—hellbent on making sure that the prophecy of forgiveness would never come to pass. Their leader, a nasty piece of work called Verchiel, wanted him dead in the worst of ways, but Aaron just couldn't find it in his heart to oblige.

"It's that no-dogs-allowed thing again, isn't it?" the Lab interrupted Aaron's thoughts again, frustrated by the fact that he couldn't eat. Gabriel loved to eat—and to talk . . . and talk and talk. *"Is it because they think we smell, Aaron?"* the dog asked. *"I don't think I smell any worse than most babies do."*

Being able to understand the dog—being able to understand the language of all living things—was but one of the strengths of Aaron's Nephilim birthright. With the help of his angel mentor, Camael, and an old fallen angel called Belphegor, he had successfully merged with the power of Heaven that flowed through his body. This power provided him with the strength and skill he would need to achieve his destiny, as well as deal with the threat still posed by Verchiel and the Powers.

"I think you smell better than most babies too," he complimented the dog, "but they still won't let you eat inside. We'll have something when we get back to Aerie. Don't worry; I won't let you starve."

Aerie was their home now, a settlement of fallen angels and Nephilim dedicated to the belief in the ancient prophecy that Aaron was supposed to represent. Aerie had also become his responsibility.

The dog grumbled, not completely satisfied with the compromise, but knowing he had little choice. Aaron knew that feeling well enough. He could complain all he wanted, but it wouldn't change the fact that he had a destiny to fulfill. He tried not to allow his new duties to overwhelm him, but it was a challenge. Not only did he have to protect the citizens of Aerie, knowing that Verchiel was still out there looking for revenge, he also had to look after Vilma and deal with the most recent revelation that Lucifer was the angel who fathered him. *Who ever said that being a savior was all fun and games?*

Aaron turned away from the restaurant and looked toward the phone booth where Vilma appeared to be wrapping up her call.

"I'm worried about her," Gabriel said, putting words to Aaron's sentiments as they both watched her hang up the phone and emerge from the glass-and-metal cubicle.

Vilma had been part of Aaron's old life, before the power of the angels asserted itself and turned the world as he had known it on its ear. Although he had kept in contact through e-mail, he hadn't really thought he would ever see her again, yet another piece of his life that he was forced to abandon. But here she was, inexplicably made part of his new existence—a Nephilim too. He always felt he was in love with her, always knew there was some powerful connection, but that just made her involvement in the whirlwind that his life had become all the more scary.

"Is everything okay at home?" he asked as she approached them.

The girl shrugged, combing a nervous hand through her shiny, black shoulder-length hair. "As good as can be expected, I guess," she said, not looking at him.

She was sweating, even though the temperature wasn't above sixty degrees, and he also noticed the dark circles under her normally beautiful brown eyes.

Aaron reached out gingerly to touch Vilma's shoulder. "Are you all right?" he asked softly.

Vilma raised her face to look at him, eyes filled with emotion. "No," she answered, shaking her head as the tears began to tumble down the dark skin of her cheeks. "I've been taken away from my home and my school, been tortured by . . . monsters, I'm having dreams that make me afraid to go to sleep, and . . . and there's something coming alive inside me that I can't even begin to understand. No, Aaron, I am so *not* all right."

She was angry and scared, and he knew exactly how she felt, for it wasn't that long ago that he first experienced the awakening of the angelic essence within himself. He tried to think of the right things to say to reassure her, but he couldn't; he didn't want to lie. Aaron had no idea how things were going to be in the future—for her, for himself, for the fallen angels. Life was uncertain right now, and that was something that he was learning to live with. It was something Vilma was going to have to learn as well.

As if on cue, Gabriel leaned his large, yellow body against the girl, nudging her hand with his cold, damp nose. *"Don't cry, Vilma,"* he said consolingly, his dark eyes looking up into hers. *"Everything is going to be fine. Just you wait and see."*

She began to pat his blocky head, and Aaron could see the immediate calming effect that the dog's presence had upon her. In the week since they had saved her from Verchiel's grasp, Gabriel had become Vilma's anchor to sanity.

"I'm very tired," she said, her voice no louder than a whisper. "I think I'd like to go ho—" Vilma halted, the word catching in her throat before it could leave her mouth. She was going to say "home." But it wasn't home for her, although it would have to do until the threat of Verchiel and his Powers was ended once and for all.

"I'll take you back to Aerie," Aaron said quietly, putting his arm around her and gently pulling her close.

She nodded and said nothing more as Gabriel, too, stepped closer.

Using another of the gifts from his angelic nature, Aaron willed them all invisible, then allowed the massive, shiny black wings to unfurl from his back. He thought of Aerie, picturing in his mind the abandoned neighborhood built atop a burial ground for toxic waste, enfolded Vilma and Gabriel within his feathered embrace, and took them there.

Deep within the hold of oblivion, Lucifer had sought the escape of torment, and instead found memories of times preferred forgotten.

He saw it all as he always did when he closed his eyes: the crimes he committed against God, the war he waged in Heaven in the name of petty jealousy. But when those recollections were spent, the wounds of his past discretion reopened, the first of the fallen saw that the painful conjurings of his mind were not yet finished with him.

It had been years since he last dreamed of her—thought of her—and he moaned in protest as remembrances long suppressed played out upon his dreamscape. Her name was Taylor, and the memory of her was as painful as anything he'd been forced to endure since his capture by Verchiel and his followers.

He saw her as he had that very first time: a beautiful, human woman who emanated life and vitality, with rich, dark eyes the color of polished mahogany, and jet-black hair that curled seductively around her shoulders. She was wearing a flowing yellow sundress, leather sandals upon her delicate feet, and she was playing with a dog—a golden retriever named Brandy. There was something about her that drew him in, something that made him believe he might not be the monster his own kind had branded him to be.

In the brief time that he had been with her, Lucifer had almost been able to convince himself that he was just a man, not the leader of a rebellion against God. How beautifully mundane his life had become, the urge to wander the planet, as he had done for thousands of years, suddenly stifled by the love of an earthly woman. It was as if she had been touched by the Archons themselves; there was an inherent magick in her that seemed to calm his restless spirit and numb the pain of the curse he would forever carry as the inciter of Heaven's war.

Lucifer fought toward consciousness, but the current of the past was too strong, and he was drowned in further memories, pulled deeper. It was in fact the dreams that had been harbingers to the end of his happiness with the woman. He had begun to experience dreams of the turmoil for which he was responsible, of the blood and death—the faces of those who had died for his cause haunting his attempts at peace. The dreams were relentless. They reawakened in him the enormity of his sins, and he knew that he must move on. He had not yet earned the right to peace and happiness. How stupid he had been to think that his penance might be at an end. Though it pained him, he left her—the beautiful, magickal Taylor—and began his wanderings anew.

And in his fevered mind he saw her as he had that very last time, asleep in the bed they'd shared as man and woman. How beautiful she was. He had left her during the night, sneaking silently out into the darkness and out of her life. It was for the best, he had told himself, for he could bring her nothing but misery.

But this time the memory was different and he did not leave. Instead Taylor stirred upon the bed, as if feeling his gaze upon her, and she rolled over to look at him, a seductive smile spreading across her features, clad in the shadows of the early hour.

"Hello, Lucifer," she said in a voice filled with the huskiness of interrupted sleep, and he felt his love for the woman swell within him.

It was as if he had never left her.

chapter two

Lorelei sighed as the commotion continued to escalate. She placed her hands flat atop the table, took a deep breath, and forced herself not to utter an incantation that would have called down lightning from the sky and permanently silenced the agitated citizens gathered in the meeting room of Aerie's community center.

"People, please," she said, raising her voice to be heard above their frenetic din. "We'll get absolutely nothing accomplished here if we're all talking at once."

The citizens ignored her and continued their excited chatter, the volume within the low-ceilinged room intensifying. She remembered how easy it had seemed for Belphegor to preside over these meetings. All the ancient fallen angel had to do was stand up from his chair and clear his throat, and immediately they would all fall silent, awaiting his words with rapt attention. And that was just one of the things she missed about their leader.

Belphegor had been mortally injured during the Powers' attack upon Aerie, in a violent duel with their commander, Verchiel. They had found him close to death, but Aaron Corbet had set him free from his shell of flesh and blood, forgiving him and all the others that had fallen in the devastating battle, allowing them to return to Heaven. Lorelei had been happy for them; it was what every one of the fallen inhabiting this place dreamed of, but Belphegor's absence was felt each and every day.

"There's been enough talk," said a fallen angel named Atliel. He was standing up beside his metal folding chair, his single eye and badly burned face commanding the attention of those around him. The angel had been scarred in the battle with the Powers, but at least he had survived when so many others of the citizenry had not.

Lorelei looked about the room and was reminded of how many had been lost trying to defend Aerie from Verchiel's soldiers. Not all of them died; Aaron had freed many fallen angels who had managed to hang on to a thread of life. Even still, their numbers had been cut easily by half, and that didn't count those Nephilim who had been seriously injured. They were still trying to heal, the question of their survival nowhere near certain.

"We must act at once or suffer the fate of our brothers," Atliel proclaimed, looking about the room, his scarred visage quieting the congregation far more effectively than had Lorelei's raised voice.

"And what do you propose?" the Nephilim asked, rising from her chair as she'd seen Belphegor do in the past, hoping she could regain some control of the meeting. She knew many of the citizens were not happy that she, a Nephilim, a half-breed, had assumed control of the angelic settlement with their founder's passing, but it had been Belphegor's wish. His confidence in her ability to lead had always surpassed her own. Even though the fallen angels and the Nephilim lived together in relative harmony, there was still a certain amount of prejudice—especially when it came to the decisions that would govern the future of Aerie.

Atliel turned to fix her in the gaze of his good eye. It was obvious that he didn't appreciate her interruption. "We must do what we have in the past when we've been threatened," he answered, a hint of petulance in his voice. "Aerie must be relocated. We cannot chance another Powers attack."

Lorelei watched the reactions of those before her. They were a mixture of shock, quiet acceptance, and complete despair. Aerie had been in many places throughout the millennia it had existed, moving from one secret location to the next as the Powers grew closer to finding them. To many of the sanctuary's newer residents, the abandoned neighborhood of the Ravenschild Estates was the only true home they had ever known, and that she knew from personal experience.

"Don't you think we've come too far for that?" she asked, stoking the fires of Atliel's ire. "Do you think that Belphegor and all the other citizens who fell during the battle did so only that we could run and hide again? I seriously doubt it."

Atliel gripped the edge of the chair in front of him, knuckles white with the force of his frustration. "Verchiel and his followers know where we are. They can return at any moment to finish what they started. Aerie must survive if we are ever to find forgiveness from our Father in Heaven. Nothing else matters."

Lorelei moved out from behind the table. She knew they were afraid, but she couldn't believe that they were so blinded by their fear that they didn't see the signs of change that were upon them, changes that had begun soon after Aaron Corbet had arrived in Aerie.

"I believe the time you've been waiting for, the forgiveness you've been seeking, is upon us, Atliel," she said, leaning back against the table edge and crossing her booted feet at the ankles.

"You're referring to that Nephilim, Aaron Corbet," the fallen angel responded, a sneer upon his damaged features.

"Yes," she replied emphatically, "I am."

Atliel slowly shook his head. "The savior of prophecy," he grumbled, looking at those gathered around him. "I'm having great difficulty believing that—"

"You saw what he can do," Lorelei cried, pushing away from the table to stress her point. "You saw what he did for Camael—what he did for Belphegor and all the others who fell in battle."

"Yes, but—"

"He *forgave* them," Lorelei continued over Atliel's protest. She didn't have the patience for his or any of the others' doubts. Aaron Corbet was the *One*, and she wasn't about to let a discordant voice among them detract from what was finally, after thousands and thousands of years, about to happen to them. "Aaron allowed them to return to Heaven, and I believe he'll do the same for you."

The room was suddenly quiet and Lorelei saw that all eyes were finally upon her. She was proud of herself for speaking out. The citizens of Aerie could no longer allow themselves to be governed by fear. These were new times ahead of them, and they needed a fresh perspective.

"And where is our savior?" Atliel posed his question to the room at large. "Was he not made aware of this gathering?"

"Yes, he was, but—"

It was Atliel's turn to interrupt as a low buzz moved through the crowd. "He was aware, but he chose not to attend. Is that what you're telling us, Lorelei? That the fate of our hopes and dreams is teetering on the edge of a precipice, and Aaron Corbet could not be bothered?"

"Look," she began, exasperated—by Aaron's unexplained absence, by Atliel's persistent questioning, by her own lack of control. "All I'm saying is that we need to consider all our options before we turn tail and run. At least talk to Aaron, he might be able to give us—"

"And all I'm asking, Lorelei," Atliel said, cutting her off again, "is for our *savior* to start acting like one and offer us some guidance."

She didn't know how to respond, choosing instead to say nothing, and in a matter of moments the commotion was on the rise again, voices of fallen angels and Nephilim alike, all speaking at once, clamoring to be heard.

Shit, Aaron thought, suddenly remembering the meeting at Aerie's community center that he had promised Lorelei he would attend.

He was in the process of transporting Vilma, Gabriel, and himself back to their house in Aerie, traversing the void between *here* and *there*. It was one of the few angelic skills that he genuinely appreciated. All he had to do was picture in his mind the place he wished to be, wrap himself within his wings, and in a matter of seconds he was there. In this particular instant, though, he was forced to change his mind mid-trip, and he opened his wings to emerge on the street in front of the community center.

"I'm really sorry about this," he apologized to his traveling companions as his wings receded beneath the flesh of his back. "I just remembered that I promised Lorelei I'd go to the community meeting today and . . ."

Vilma smiled weakly, and he couldn't get over how tired she looked. "That's okay," she said. "I think I need to lie down anyway. I'm still feeling pretty exhausted."

Aaron glanced over at the entrance to the community center and caught Lehash sitting out front, watching them. The fallen angel in charge of Aerie's security tipped his cowboy hat in greeting, looking every inch as though he'd just walked out of an old spaghetti Western. Aaron smiled and waved briefly before turning his attention back to Vilma.

"Gabriel will go with you," he told the girl.

She reached down and scratched the top of the Lab's bony head. "Is that what you want to do, Gabe?" she asked him in the language of dogs.

"Will you give me breakfast?"

"Of course I will," she assured him.

"Then let's go," Gabriel said, already beginning to walk in the direction of the house where they were staying. *"I'm starving."*

Vilma laughed, then paused to look back at Aaron.

"I'll see you later?" she asked, and he could hear the sadness permeating her voice.

It just about broke his heart. *But it won't last forever,* he tried to reassure himself. He stepped toward her and put his arms tentatively around her. "It's going to be all right," he whispered in her ear, squeezing her tightly.

Vilma hugged him back, but said nothing to prove that she believed in what he had told her.

"C'mon, Vilma. Let's go," Gabriel called, his tail wagging eagerly as he urged her to follow.

She was the first to break the embrace, looking deeply into Aaron's eyes and forcing a smile before turning to join the dog.

It's an enormous adjustment, he told himself, watching as she walked away from him. *She just needs time.* He could sense the angelic essence inside her becoming stronger, and prayed for an easy merger. Hopefully it wouldn't take much longer for the process to complete itself.

Aaron turned and jogged toward the community center. "Lorelei is going to kill me," he said to the fallen angel that just happened to be her father.

Lehash had tipped his chair back on two legs and was leaning against the building's wall. "Not sure you want to be going in there right now," he said in the drawl of the Old West. "Folks are a mite riled up at the moment. Lorelei's attempting to calm 'em down."

"What are they upset about?"

"You," Lehash answered, lowering his chair legs to the ground.

"Me?" Aaron asked incredulously.

The fallen angel nodded. "Yep. They're worried that yer not taking the job of savior seriously enough." The angel gunslinger tilted back the brim of his hat and looked into Aaron's eyes. "They want to know why you haven't got around to savin' them yet."

"Son of a bitch," Aaron hissed as he grabbed hold of the handle and flung the door wide.

"What're you gonna do?" he heard Lehash call after him as he stormed inside.

"I'm going to have a little talk with the citizens of Aerie."

Lehash guffawed, his chair sliding across the ground as he abruptly stood, following the Nephilim into the building.

"This I gotta see," Aaron heard the angel say.

Aaron entered the meeting room through a door at the back and immediately felt as though he was in the midst of one of those bizarre go-to-school-naked dreams. He had heard them carrying on as he approached, each trying to be heard above the other and Lorelei shouting for order.

And they did quiet down, but only because they saw that he had arrived.

Every head swiveled in his direction, and every eye watched as he strode down the aisle to join Lorelei at the front. He didn't make eye contact with any of them, but could sense their hostility and their frustration. The feelings were mutual.

"Sorry I'm late," he said quietly to Lorelei as she stepped aside to allow him her space.

He faced the crowded room. Lehash was standing at the back, arms folded, leaning against the wall, a sly smile on his haggard features. They were all there—Nephilim and fallen angels both. And why shouldn't they be? The citizens of Aerie were concerned about their future, a future in which Aaron played a large part. It was a heavy responsibility, and he felt as though he was beginning to buckle beneath its tremendous weight. He was doing the best he could, but sometimes it just didn't seem to be enough.

"Sorry I'm late," he said again to the room at large.

But before he could continue, Atliel interrupted. "Aerie must be relocated," he declared, his single eye staring intensely. "We cannot risk any more lives. The dream of Aerie must survive, and it cannot if we stay here."

"I don't think we need to worry about Verchiel right now," Aaron tried to reassure the citizens. "He suffered casualties even greater than ours, thanks to Lorelei here. I believe we're safe for now." He looked to Lorelei for support, and saw that she was nodding in agreement.

"*You* believe we're safe?" Atliel said pointing a long finger at him.

Aaron cringed. He didn't want this to turn into an argument. He had wanted to come in, tell them what he had planned for their future, and then spend the remainder of the day with Vilma. "Yes, *I* do."

The angel's expression turned to one of complete revulsion. "What right have you to tell us we'll be safe, when you know very well what Verchiel is capable of?"

He felt his heart rate quicken, his blood beginning to rush through his veins. He forced himself to stay calm. It was a democracy here in Aerie, and the citizens had every right to speak their minds.

"He killed your parents," Atliel snarled. "Turned your little brother into a monster. Killed your mentor and used your woman as bait to lure you to your death."

Aaron knew all this. It was with him every day, a constant reminder of how much his life had changed—of what his destiny as a savior had taken from him.

"Verchiel is an unpredictable force," Atliel continued. "All of us have feared his wrath since our fall from Heaven. Do not tell me that we're safe. It couldn't be further from the truth."

Aaron's anger was growing and he felt the power of his angelic heritage course through his blood and muscle, enflaming the very essence of his being. "I'm doing my best," he said through gritted teeth. He saw that Lehash had moved away from the wall and was approaching the front. The warrior angel obviously suspected that something was about to happen, and he couldn't have been more right.

"We of Aerie expect more from our savior than his *best*." And with those words, Atliel spread his wings, as did some others in the community center, and they began to flap gently in unison, the close confines of the meeting space filled with the sound of feathered wings striking the air. They did it to show their displeasure, to show their doubt that Aaron was capable of fulfilling the prophecy.

The sigils rose to the surface of his skin and Aaron knew that he could hold back his anger no longer. He let out a cry of rage as his ebony wings exploded from his back, and he too began to beat the air, harder, singularly drowning out the sounds of the others. He watched the expressions of shock and surprise spread across the faces of the citizens as he revealed to them the shape of their redeemer. His mighty wings continued to flap, forcing them back, tipping over their chairs and creating a mini-maelstrom of dust and dirt.

And as abruptly as he had started, he stopped, furling his appendages at his back and glaring at them all.

"Why don't you people just cut me some slack?" His voice rumbled like the growl of a dangerous, jungle beast, filled with the potential for violence. "Do you seriously believe that I understand what it means to be a savior? Well, in case you haven't figured it out yet, I don't have a clue."

Fallen angels and Nephilim alike were silent. Even Atliel had decided that it might be best to hold his tongue. Lehash stood nearby and Aaron could see sparks of golden fire dancing around his hands, the gunslinger ready to call forth his pistols of heavenly flame if necessary.

"All I'm asking is for you to give me a break. I know that you're scared—I'm scared too—but it isn't going to do anybody any good to come after me for not living up to your expectations."

Aaron made eye contact with them and they each looked away, accepting his position as top dog.

"I have no idea what tomorrow holds for me or for you. But I do know that to guarantee any future at all, we have to work together. We can't *run* from Verchiel; we have to *deal* with him." He let his wings recede beneath his flesh as the sigils began to fade.

"And that's exactly what I intend to do," he declared with finality as he strode from the room.

"Meeting adjourned."

chapter three

The tiny rodent cowered in a pocket of shadow, watching with wide, fear-filled eyes, as its friend was tortured.

It wanted to run, to flee the ugly scene, but for a reason its tiny brain could not begin to fathom, the mouse would not leave the man who had befriended it. *Man?* it questioned. Its primitive thought process grappled with the concept, for this being was far more than just a man.

It remembered the first time that it had seen him. It was living in a monastery in mountains far, far away, and Lucifer arrived in the midst of a terrific snowstorm. The brothers who dwelt in the monastery had no idea how he had made it to their door, but they welcomed him inside, inviting him to share their evening meal. He had claimed to be a traveler, grown weary from his wanderings, looking for a place to rest and reflect upon a life filled with regrets. The brothers offered their monastery as a refuge and Lucifer accepted their offer to stay.

The mouse watched as the five beings that abused its friend hoisted him up, naked, into the air, hanging him from thick black chains secured upon his wrists and ankles, his face pointed at the floor. They crouched beneath him, carefully examining his exposed underbelly.

When first they met, the stranger had asked of the mouse a favor. Lucifer spoke to it in the language of its species and gave it a delicious piece of bread as payment. He had simply asked it to keep its eyes open when wandering about the monastery, and to let him know if it saw any strangers like himself. A relationship was born that benefited them both greatly, and soon blossomed into something larger, a mutual admiration—a genuine friendship.

The tiny observer watched an Archon stand beneath its hanging friend, and in his hand, there formed a knife of flame. With one sudden, savage movement, the Archon cut open its friend, his blood raining down to puddle upon the floor.

It wanted to help its friend, but instead retreated farther into the darkness of the corner. For what could it possibly do?

It was only a mouse.

† † †

The rite was forbidden. Archon Oraios was sure of that. But here they were, making preparations to reverse the Word of God.

"Quickly!" Archon Jao screeched, crouching beneath the body of the first of the fallen as the prisoner's blood poured from the gash cut into his belly. "Bring me the bowl. We cannot waste a drop!"

Archon Domiel retrieved a golden ceremonial bowl from their belongings and carefully slid it beneath the dripping wound of the hanging Lucifer.

"Excellent," Jao said rubbing his long, spidery hands together as he watched the spattering of warm crimson begin to fill the bowl. "There is much to be done with this blood. Every drop must serve our master's cause."

Archon Oraios turned his gaze from the unconscious Lucifer to Jao beside him. "Is that what he is to us now, brother?" the angel asked. "When first we joined Verchiel's quest to rid the world of God's offenders, we did so as equals, sharing the Powers' abhorrence for those who had sinned against Heaven. But now it appears we are nothing more than servants to his rage."

"Careful, Oraios," Archon Jaldabaoth warned, on hands and knees, dipping his fingers into the bowl of gore upon the floor. "Remember the fate of our brothers, Sabaoth and Erathaol. Their actions did not please Verch . . . our master, and for that they paid a price most dear." Jaldabaoth began to paint a large circle of blood on the hardwood floor beneath the first of the fallen angels.

"Why can't you say it, brother?" Oraios asked. "Paid a price most dear, indeed," he snarled. "Verchiel killed them in a fit of anger. It seems that our *master* has become quite enamored with the act of murder."

Archon Domiel turned away with a hiss. "I do not want to hear this," he said, shaking his head. "Sacrifices must be made to achieve one's ultimate goals. Verchiel's cause is a just one, a final attempt to right a grievous wrong."

The air was thick with the smell of blood as Jao joined Jaldabaoth on the floor. "This discussion is finished," he said, dipping his fingers in the collected blood of their enemy and completing the circle. "There is far too much to be done to debate this now."

"The killing of our Malakim pedagogue—with more to follow if we are to have what we need to complete the rite to unravel the words of the Most Holy and unleash Hell upon the world. Is that how a grievous wrong is righted, my Archon brothers?" Oraios asked, ignoring Jao.

"It is too late to be thinking of such things," Katspiel said quietly from the far corner. Slowly he lifted his head, the shadows of the room flowing to fill the empty sockets of his eyes like oil. In an earlier ritual he had attempted to look upon the Hell within Lucifer, and had paid the price with his sight. "Events have transpired beyond our abilities to control," he wheezed. "We are just cogs in the great mechanism that has been set in motion."

"So you say we are to continue as we are," Oraios asked his eyeless brother, "carrying out the wants and desires of one who could very well damn us all."

"Yes," Katspiel said, his head slipping forward as he began to drift off into the meditative slumber that would allow him to locate the next of the Malakim. "But I would not concern yourself with potential damnation, Brother Oraios.

"For what we have done, and are about to do, we are already damned."

Verchiel stood naked before the healer, allowing the blind human to administer to his injuries, both old and new.

The rich smell of ancient oils wafted up as Kraus dipped cloths into his restorative medicament and gently applied them to the Powers leader's various lesions.

"I apologize for the pain I must be causing, my lord," the human said. "But I must try a stronger remedy if I am ever to mend your wounds completely."

Verchiel's injuries were extensive and were healing far more slowly than normal for an angel of such power. Some were not healing at all. *Another piece of evidence that the Holy Creator has indeed abandoned His most faithful soldier,* he thought bitterly, the agony of the healing oils nothing in comparison to being forsaken.

The leader of the Powers host shuddered as his servant applied more of the medicinal balm.

"If only I could share your pain, my master," Kraus said as he bowed his head in sadness. "I would gladly bear the burden to lessen your suffering."

Verchiel gazed down upon the lesser being kneeling at his feet. "The path before us is fraught with danger," the angel said, laying his hand upon the human's head. "The potential for injuries most excruciating is great. Do you still wish to partake of my pain, little monkey?"

Kraus lifted his head to gaze upon Verchiel with sightless eyes bulging white, his old face twisted in adoration. "It would be the least I could do," Kraus said, his body trembling. "But since I cannot bear your pain, I will soothe your injuries and heal your wounds for as long as the gift of life still fills these bones and I am allowed to serve you."

Verchiel thought of his own master and what Verchiel had lost. How he had loved his Creator, but obviously it wasn't enough to prevent Him from turning away—from bestowing His blessings upon the most wretched of creations, the criminals and the mongrel abominations. The angel seethed with anger. He wanted to lash out—to rend and tear, to burn to ashes anything and everything that reminded him of his loss.

A faint wheeze pulled the leader of the Powers from his distraught reverie, and he saw that he had grabbed the blind human by the throat and was squeezing the life from his body. The monkey thrashed in his grip, but the look of rapture, of pure adoration, was still upon his face.

Verchiel let the healer fall from his angry hand, for it was not the fault of this lowly life form that the Creator had chosen to desert him.

The blind healer struggled for breath as he lay upon the floor of the old classroom. "So sorry," he gasped over and over again, certain that he had done something to offend his master.

But the monkey's apologies—his solicitations for forgiveness—would not fall upon deaf ears, as Verchiel's had. He would hear his servant's pleadings, and he would answer.

Verchiel unfurled his wings and knelt beside his quivering supplicant. "I hear your pleas," he said as he took the frightened man into his arms and drew him close. "But you have nothing to be sorry for."

Kraus began to cry, moisture leaking from his sightless orbs.

"It was *my* rage, my own inner turmoil, that almost caused your death," Verchiel said to him. "And for that error *I* am sorry."

The pain of his injuries was suddenly gone

and Verchiel was filled with the power of his own divinity. He knew then, truly understood what it was like to be a god—blessed with the power of damnation or absolution.

"I will show you the depth of my regret," the angel said, drawing the still trembling Kraus closer. Verchiel leaned his head forward and placed a gentle kiss upon each milky, cataract-covered orb.

And the healer began to scream.

The pain was like nothing Kraus had ever experienced.

He fell away from his master's embrace, stumbling about the classroom as the pain in his useless eyes intensified. He had memorized the layout of the room, as well as the entire abandoned Saint Athanasius Church and Orphanage where the Powers were gathered these days, but sheer panic and roiling pain made him careless. He ran headlong into a wall, falling to the floor in a quivering heap.

Why would he do this to me? Kraus's thoughts raced. *Have I insulted him?* He wanted to ask his master, but his distress was too great. It felt as though molten metal had been poured into his eye sockets, and instead of cooling with the passage of time, it was growing hotter and hotter still.

He thought he was going to die.

Kraus curled up on the floor and waited for

death to take him. The torment was so great that he thought he might actually welcome the end to his pitiful existence. Eyes tightly clenched, a ball of shivering blood, bone, and flesh, he readied himself—and then he heard the voice of his master. It drifted upon the air like the notes of the most beautiful song he had ever heard.

"Open your eyes."

And Kraus did as he was told. The pain was gone, but he barely noticed.

He could see!

He was gazing at the floor. It was wood, covered with decades of dirt and dust. And Kraus was seeing it all for the very first time, the intricacies, patterns and colors of the wood, and the accumulated filth. Somehow, even though he had never seen before, having been blind since birth, he knew what he was looking at, the identity of each thing his new eyes fell upon filling his head.

"Lift your head from the ground and gaze upon the world," the angel Verchiel said, his voice booming around the room. "This is my gift to you."

Kraus looked up, his new sight landing on the wall above the floor. It was painted a dingy gray; and above that was a blackboard, the faint trace of the last lesson taught within the schoolroom still evident upon its dark surface. *Thou shalt not kill*, he read, despite never having learned to read.

Everything his new vision saw, all the colors, the shapes, the items left behind when the school was abandoned, he knew their identity, their purpose, and was filled with the wonder of it all.

The air stirred behind him and Kraus turned to *see* for the first time the creature that had given him this most wonderful gift. How blessed he was to serve an emissary of God, so merciful as to heal a lowly beast such as he. His master stood before him, naked, mighty wings spread wide so that he might gaze upon the full glory of the angel, of Heaven embodied.

And Kraus genuinely saw the master that he had served these many years. The scars of battle, the burns—seeping and red—and the wings, now gone to seed, molted, and the color of grime.

"I am the glory of Heaven," Verchiel proclaimed.

But the healer, once blind, now saw his master for what he truly was.

He saw a monster.

chapter four

Aaron stepped out of the community center, the lingering sensation of his transformation still causing his flesh to tingle. He remembered a time not too long ago when a change from his human form to the angelic would have caused him nothing but pain. Now it had become almost second nature, the two halves of his being, opposite sides to the same coin.

He took a few calming, deep breaths. The air was surprisingly cool, despite the fact that April was almost over. Yes, there had been some warm days, but it seemed that winter was having a difficult time abdicating its seasonal seat of power.

Gradually he began to feel the tension leaving his body. Aaron never expected being a savior was going to be easy, but he wished that the citizens of Aerie would give him a chance to figure things out at his own speed. Decisions as gravely important as what to do about Verchiel just couldn't be rushed. There was too much at stake.

"Damn," said a familiar voice from behind, and Aaron turned to see Lehash approaching. "Guess you gave them a little somethin' to chew on," he said, a big smile spreading across his usually dour features as he motioned with his thumb toward the door behind him.

"They made me mad," Aaron said, sounding trite and not at all proud of his reaction.

"No kiddin'," Lehash said with a rumbling chuckle. "Wish Belphegor was here to see you put old Atliel and his cronies in their places. It would've made him happier than a pig in slop."

Aaron chuckled as well. "I guess it's not how you'd expect a messiah to act."

The angel withdrew a thin cigar from inside his duster pocket and lit it with the tip of his leather-gloved forefinger. "Hell, boy, you put Verchiel down for the count and get us back to Heaven, you can act any way you damn well please."

Sensing that they were no longer alone, both Aaron and Lehash turned to see the citizens leaving the community center. Atliel and his cronies stood to the side of the building's entrance glaring at them.

"I think somebody's gettin' the hairy eyeball," Lehash said, sucking on the end of his cigar and blowing a cloud of smoke up into the air. "And I don't think it's me."

"What do you think I should do?" Aaron asked the gunslinger, his voice at a whisper. "Should I apologize or just let it go?"

The fallen angel rolled the cigar around in his mouth. "Personally, I'd let 'em stew, but then again, I ain't no messiah. You're gonna haf'ta do what you think is right."

Aaron's foster dad had taught him that nine out of ten times it was easier to apologize and move past the problem. Tom Stanley had been a good man and a wonderful father, and Aaron missed him very much. He decided he would honor the memory of the only father he had ever known by doing what *he* would have thought was right.

Aaron moved around Lehash and walked toward the gaggle of fallen angels. "Look, I'm sorry for my behavior in there," he said with genuine sincerity. If he was going to be their leader, he guessed that it probably wouldn't hurt for them to see that he knew he wasn't infallible and could admit when he was wrong. "Things have been kind of crazy for me and I just wanted to—"

"Is it true what they're saying?" Atliel suddenly interrupted. "I thought it was only a wild rumor, but seeing you in there, the anger you wield, I can almost believe it to be true."

His three companions nodded their agreement.

"I don't understand," Aaron said. "What rumors are you talking about?"

Atliel looked to his brethren for support and then back to Aaron, bolstered by their admiration. "That you are the son of the Morningstar— the spawn of Lucifer," he spat.

Aaron didn't know how to respond. He knew what he had been told, but he couldn't yet bring himself to believe it. "I . . . I'm not sure that . . . ," he stuttered.

"See how he responds," Atliel said to his comrades. "It *is* true that we are to be delivered to salvation by the progeny of the monster who led us to our fall."

Lehash moved forward, a pistol of heavenly fire glistening gold in his gloved hand. "That'll be enough of that, brother," the law of Aerie said, stepping between the Nephilim and the group of angels.

"It's okay, Lehash," Aaron said quickly. "They're right in their concern. How *are* they supposed to trust the son of the Devil to lead them to salvation?" he asked quietly as he turned away. Though he had no desire to, and had been avoiding it for days, Aaron Corbet knew that he had to confront the mystery of his heritage before he could finally assume his role as Aerie's savior.

Vilma mistook the sudden wave of panic as another example of the angelic essence awakening, but as she and Gabriel entered the ranch-style house she shared with Lorelei and Lehash, she remembered that this was senior finals week at school. The feeling was sudden, like an electrical jolt, and her entire body broke out in a tingling sweat. It didn't take her long to realize that this had nothing to do with the power residing inside her, and everything to do with her academic career crumbling to ruin.

She slammed the door behind her, and Gabriel started from the noise.

"Are you okay?" the Labrador asked, his head tilted to the right with concern.

"I'm fine," she answered with a sigh. "Sorry I slammed the door."

"That's okay," he said, walking past her, toward the kitchen. He turned and looked at her. *"How about breakfast now?"*

Grateful for the distraction, Vilma filled the dog's bowl with food and got him some fresh water. "Here you go," she said, stepping back and watching him devour his meal in record time. He licked his chops, took a long, slurping drink, and then cleaned his bowl with his tongue.

"Happy?" she asked as she followed him into the living room.

"Yes, thank you." Gabriel hopped up onto the couch and turned once in a circle before settling down to rest. *"I need a nap, though."* He exhaled noisily and closed his eyes.

Vilma shook her head, watching him for a moment. She had never owned a dog and was amazed by how much Gabriel slept. This was but one of many naps he'd take during the day before going to bed and sleeping through the night. Aaron always joked that it was Gabriel's job to sleep, and if the animal could collect a check for snoozing, they'd both be millionaires.

She sat down in a large, overstuffed chair and pulled her knees up to her chin. She felt cold inside, but it had nothing to do with the actual temperature. She was afraid again. Until a month ago, she knew exactly what she was going to do with her life: finish high school, go on to college for a degree in education, and then teach, preferably first or second grade.

She smiled sadly, remembering how she would talk with her friends about the future, and how excited it made her. They thought she was a freak, never really understanding that this was the stuff that made her truly happy, that this was as exciting for her as they found dancing at the all-ages club or conning someone into buying them liquor. Her plans for the future were her hopes and dreams, and everything was going fabulously until she met Aaron Corbet.

Vilma's anger flared. She didn't want to blame him for her troubles, but it was so easy. What would have happened if she hadn't spoken to him that day at the library? She sat with her chin atop her knees, rocking from side to side, thinking about what her life would be like without him. She tried desperately to believe that it would have been better, but deep down she knew that wasn't true. She had felt a strange attraction to him the first time she noticed him at his locker across from hers, as if their being together was part of some bigger plan. And when Aaron had gone away after the deaths of his foster family, Vilma had never felt so lonely—so incomplete.

And now they were together again, but still she felt lonely and frightened, although she knew Aaron was doing the best he could to help her adjust to the changes in her life.

Something stirred inside her, but this time the sensation had nothing to do with anxiety. The angelic power, stirred too quickly to maturity by the tortures of Verchiel, was awake again, and she felt it testing the confines of the flesh and blood that was its cage.

Aaron had tried to explain that the essence had been a part of her since her conception, that the power had simply lain dormant within her, waiting for her to come of age and embrace it. For most Nephilim the unification of the human and heavenly sides was a naturally occurring process, but for others . . .

Vilma didn't want to think about it anymore. The idea of the thing inside her was driving her insane. She dropped her feet to the floor and quickly stood, looking about the room for something, anything, that could distract her.

Gabriel came awake, lifting his head slowly to stare at her.

"I'm sorry, Gabriel," Vilma said, nervously biting at the cuticles of one of her fingers. "I'm feeling a bit antsy. I need to do something—to get my mind off things for a while." She remembered she'd only had a piece of toast earlier that morning, and thought that food would be as good a distraction as anything. "I'm going to get something to eat, want to come?" She knew it was a stupid question, for the Lab was *always* hungry.

"Don't mind if I do," he said, quickly getting down from the sofa and following her to the small kitchen where he had eaten a full meal only minutes before.

Vilma went to the fridge and opened the door, peering inside at some vegetables and milk of questionable age. Gabriel squeezed his head past her leg to take a look for himself.

"Hmmm," he grumbled. *"Nothing good in here."*

The power inside her had calmed, but it was still awake. She could feel it experiencing the world through her actions. She closed the refrigerator and looked around the kitchen. In a wicker basket by the sink she spotted some red delicious apples.

"How about an apple?" she asked the dog as she plucked the largest one from the basket.

"I love apples." Gabriel had already begun to drool.

Vilma grabbed a knife from a drawer and cut the apple in half. "Do you eat the skin or do you want me to peel it for you?"

"The skin is fine," he said, wagging his tail, a puddle forming on the floor beneath his leaking mouth. *"Just take the core out, please. The seeds make me choke."*

Vilma held half of the apple in one hand and sank the tip of the knife into the fruit to cut away the core as she had done for her nieces and nephews countless times before. It was then that the angelic essence chose to exert itself, surging forward to throw itself against the prison of her body. She gasped aloud as the knife blade sank through the flesh of the apple and into the palm of her hand. Bleeding, she dropped both to the kitchen floor. But all she could do was tremble, watching as the scarlet fluid oozed from the wound in her palm, running down her arm.

The power was shrieking inside her, aroused by the spilling of her own blood, and no matter how many calming thoughts she tried to put into her head, the angelic force continued to build. She couldn't hold it back; it was exactly what she feared.

"Vilma!" Gabriel cried, moving toward her, trying to calm her as he'd done in the past. But he was too late, and the power was too strong.

God help her, it was free.

Aaron approached the rundown house with trepidation.

Scholar had been asking to see him for days, but Aaron always found some reason to avoid meeting with Aerie's keeper of information and the chronicler of its history. Aaron knew the angel was right. He had come a long way in the past few weeks, but he still had much to learn— about the prophecy that he embodied and the fallen angel that had sired him.

Lucifer.

He climbed the porch steps and knocked on the door. While he had come to accept his destiny, Aaron still didn't want to believe that his father was the Devil. But he owed it to the citizens of Aerie at least to hear the proof of his heritage. If he was going to lead and expect them to follow, he had to have all of his facts straight.

Aaron knocked a second time, but there was still no answer. He briefly entertained the idea of coming back later, but knew that if he left, the chances he'd be back any time soon were slim. *No*, he thought, grabbing the doorknob and turning it. *I have to do this now.*

The door opened and a cool gust of heavily scented air reached out to greet him. The air smelled of paper, of old books. It reminded him of the basement stacks at the Lynn Public Library. There was something strangely comforting about the aroma, bringing back memories of the days when finishing a term paper and getting a good grade were the most stressful things in his life.

Aaron stepped inside and stopped in disbelief. The single room in which he stood was huge. For as far as his eyes could see, there were bookcases and piles of books of every conceivable size and shape. He thought his eyes might be playing tricks on him, for it seemed as though the inside of this house was all one room and at least five times larger than it appeared to be on the outside. He considered going out the door and coming back in.

Scholar came out from behind one of the shelves, dressed in his customary crisp white shirt—buttoned to the collar—and black pants, his face buried in an ancient tome. "I thought I heard someone knocking," he said without looking up. He continued to walk through the room, somehow managing to avoid the precariously stacked books all around him. "Come in, come in," he urged, sounding impatient. "I should have known you'd come just when I'd gotten busy with something else."

Aaron moved farther into the enormous storeroom of knowledge. "Sorry," he apologized. "If you want, I'll come back another time, when you're not so busy."

Scholar finally tore his gaze from his book, a petulant smile on his pale, gaunt face. "Tell me, when will I ever *not* be busy?"

Aaron threw up his hands. "I don't know. I was just being polite."

"Savior to us all and manners to boot," Scholar said sharply as he closed his book and placed it atop a pile already nearly five feet tall.

The pile teetered but did not fall. Strangely enough, it seemed that the laws of physics didn't apply here.

Aaron again looked about the enormous room, at the domed ceiling at least twenty feet high. "Is it me or is this place bigger than it looks outside?"

A teakettle's shrill whistle punctuated his question as Scholar motioned for him to follow. "Can't pull the wool over your eyes, can we, Aaron?" he chided. "Ancient angel magick," he explained as he walked to a small table in a far corner of the room. "Would you care for a cup?" he asked, unplugging the electric kettle and pouring the boiling water into a mug containing a tea bag. "I think there's enough water for another."

Aaron shook his head. "No, that's all right. Thanks, anyway." The last time he accepted a cup of tea from an angel it had been poisoned.

He couldn't get over the size of the room and the enormous number of books. "It's amazing how much you have here," he commented looking back to Scholar. "I never would have guessed."

The angel turned toward Aaron, blowing on the steaming liquid in his mug. "We could have filled every house in Aerie and still not had a place for it all," he said between sips. "That's when angel magick can be put to good use."

Aaron didn't remember moving, but suddenly

a stack of books tumbled over with a crash, sending three other stacks nearby to the floor as well. Scholar gasped.

"I didn't touch a thing," Aaron yelled. "Really, they just fell on their own." He made a move to start picking up the books and heard Scholar gasp all the louder.

"Please, just step away from the stacks," the fallen angel instructed, gesturing for the boy to move toward him. "That's it," he urged softly. "No sudden movements."

Aaron maneuvered himself carefully between the stacks, and noticed the angel breathe a sigh of relief as he reached him without further incident. "I'm really sorry about that," he said as Scholar helped himself to more tea.

"It's quite all right," he said with a strained smile on his pinched features. "Why don't we simply deal with the reason you have come, and then you can be on your way, hmm?"

If Aaron didn't hear it in his words, he could see in the angel's eyes that he regretted ever having invited him into his work place. But he pushed forward with his questions. "How do you know?" he asked. "How do you know for sure that . . . *he's* my father?" He didn't feel comfortable saying the name. It made him nervous, the evil connotations and all.

"Lucifer?" Scholar asked, seeming to take some kind of perverse pleasure in seeing Aaron's reaction to the name of the first of the fallen. "You showed us as much that first day we met," he explained, "when you manifested your angelic abilities, even through the manacles. Belphegor and I knew then that only an angel of enormous power could have sired one such as you."

"But aren't there other powerful angels out there that could have been with my mother? Why does it have to be—"

"The sigils," the angel interrupted, making reference to the markings that appeared on Aaron's flesh whenever he manifested the full power of his angelic heritage. "We believed that the sigils were significant to the angelic entity that sired you, but little did we imagine how much."

Aaron held out his arm and thought hard about the markings. The bare flesh began to smolder ever so slightly as the archaic shapes rose to the surface. He remembered Scholar making sketches of them at Belphegor's urgings on that first day in Aerie. Now he examined them in the flesh. "Okay, so what do they mean?" he asked.

"They are special symbols representing the names of the elite soldiers that swore their allegiance to your father and his cause," Scholar explained as he traced the shapes on Aaron's arm with the tip of his index finger. "Soldiers that died during the battle in Heaven."

Suddenly it all made sense to Aaron as he recalled the bizarre inner journey he had made with the assistance of Belphegor and a poisoned cup of tea. Within his mind, he had seen the consummation of the power that resided within him, represented by the most magnificent of angels as he bestowed his gift upon his gathered troops.

"I . . . I saw this," he stammered, looking into Scholar's intense eyes. "I saw Lucifer. . . . I saw my father. . . ."

Scholar nodded slowly, encouraging him to accept the truth. "Before the fighting began, the Morningstar gave each of his soldiers a special mark to show how important they were to him. It was with a piece of himself that he adorned them—a piece of his power."

Feeling suddenly weak, Aaron let go of the symbols and allowed them to fade from his flesh. "But why do *I* have them?" he asked, sitting down on the floor as his head swam with dizziness. "Why are they on *my* skin?"

Scholar turned away. "Belphegor and I were trying to figure that out right before Verchiel attacked," the scholarly angel said. "We believe that if Lucifer is indeed seeking absolution for his sins, then you represent his apology to God—and to all those who died for his insane cause."

Overwhelmed, Aaron buried his head in his hands as visions of the most splendorous angelic entity he could ever imagine again filled his mind. "How could anything so beautiful be responsible for so much horror?" he asked.

Scholar stood over him as Aaron sat on the floor, awash in the raw emotion of revelation. "He was afraid that he was no longer loved," he said softly gazing off into space.

"As were we all."

chapter five

"Where would we go?" Lorelei asked the angel that she had come to know as her father. The two walked down the center of the street toward the place that they called home. It was a little past noon, and on either side of them the citizens of Aerie were going about their usual business. Some were maintaining small gardens, bringing life up from the toxic soil; others simply sat in old lawn chairs, staring off into space, reflecting on all that had befallen them and what was to come.

Lehash puffed on a cigar, blowing a nasty cloud of smoke from the corner of his mouth. "What, Aerie?" he asked. "Hell if I know. Probably some abandoned wreck of a place like all the others we've picked over the millennia." He took another puff on the cheroot. "I don't know why we can't go someplace nice, like

Montana, or maybe even Texas," the gunslinger said, waxing poetic about places he had lived long ago.

"Hasn't it been a while since you've been to either of those places, Dad?" she asked, the hint of a smile tugging at the corners of her mouth.

"It's only been a couple'a hundred years or so," he commented, his eagle eyes scanning the streets of Aerie for any signs of trouble. "How much could they have changed?"

Lorelei couldn't help herself and laughed out loud. As far as Lehash was concerned, mail was still being delivered by Pony Express, and Butch Cassidy and his Wild Bunch were still robbing banks and escaping on horseback. Lorelei shook her head. She couldn't even begin to imagine the changes beings like her father had seen on Earth since their exile after Heaven's war.

"I don't want to leave here," she proclaimed, any trace of humor now gone from her voice. She motioned toward the others around them. "And I'm sure that they share my feelings as well."

The constable scratched the side of his face with his finger; it sounded as if it were made of sandpaper. "It ain't the side of an active volcano or the hull of a sunken ship, but it's served its purpose." Lehash looked about the desolate and forgotten neighborhood that was his responsibility to protect. "But if the boy manages to pull it all together, we won't be needin' to worry about whether we're gonna be stayin' here or not."

It seemed odd to hear her father talk of such things. For years Lehash's only concern had been the protection of Aerie and its people, no matter the location. Aerie was his life and his world; there was no other place for him. Heaven was something he'd given up on a long, long time ago, but that was before Aaron Corbet. The Nephilim had made him believe that the prophecy was true, that there was a chance the fallen would be forgiven, that *he* would be forgiven.

"Don't worry about me," she said bumping her shoulder against his. "You go off to Heaven, and we'll get along just fine without you."

The prophecy was vague about the fate of the Nephilim, only hinting at a special purpose for them upon the world of God's man. Lorelei felt a strange combination of fear and excitement when she thought of her own future, knowing full well that there was much to be dealt with in the present, before that long, unknown road could be traveled.

They had reached their house and were casually walking down the concrete path that led to the front door.

"I'm going to make myself a quick bite and check on Vilma. Do you want a cup of coffee or—"

Lehash had suddenly stopped, and he stood at the beginning of the path, eyes squinted as if sensing something in the air.

"Is everything okay?" she asked cautiously, moving a strand of her snow-white hair away from her face. She was beginning to feel something as well.

The door to the house blew off its hinges in an explosion of roiling fire, taking the screen door along with it. Lorelei was blown backward by the force of the blast, her ears ringing as she struggled to get to her feet.

Lehash was already moving in slow motion toward her, weapons of golden fire taking shape in his hands. Then she saw Gabriel bound through the gaping hole where the door used to be, his yellow coat black in spots and smoldering, eyes wild in panic.

"Gabriel!" she screamed as the dog ran toward them.

"*Run!*" he barked, falling to the ground and rolling to extinguish his burning fur. "*There was nothing I could do to stop it,*" the Lab cried, panting wildly. "*It's out—it's taken control of her!*"

"Son of a bitch," Lorelei heard her father mutter beneath his breath, and she looked up at the front of the house.

Vilma Santiago stood there stiffly, a corona of unnatural flame radiating from her body. "Help me," she hissed as she slowly raised her hands, watching in the grip of terror as the fires of Heaven danced upon her fingertips. She was trying to hold it back, but it had already tasted freedom and clearly wanted more.

Then Vilma's body went suddenly rigid, her eyes a glistening black, like two shiny marbles floating within a contorted expression of misery. And then that too was gone, and Vilma Santiago was suddenly no longer with them, replaced by something else altogether.

Something wild and dangerous.

Now that he had the gift of vision, Kraus half expected that his other senses, augmented by a lifetime of blindness, would begin to decline. But that wasn't the case at all. They were all just as sharp as they had been, perhaps even a bit more so with the addition of sight.

And something else had taken its place among his five senses, another feeling that warned him of dire times to come, a sensation of foreboding had become the sixth of his senses.

The healer moved about them unnoticed, still beneath their regard. He stopped to check the stitches he had sewn into the arm of a Powers soldier that perched atop the ledge of the orphanage roof. Eight others were there as well, staring silently out across western Massachusetts with dark, unwavering gazes.

"Do you feel them, brothers?" asked the warrior whose arm Kraus carefully examined, his voice leaden, as if drained of vitality. "Stirring to be born, a bane to our holy cause."

The angel was talking of Nephilim. How the Powers hated these half-breed progeny, but as of late, they had not been allowed to hunt the accursed offspring of the fallen.

"Our master tells us that there are more important concerns these days, but I, too, feel the threat of the Nephilim on the rise," said another. "I ask you, what could be more important than the extermination of these abominations?"

Infection had found its way into the angel's wound and Kraus could smell the pungent aroma of decay.

"Verchiel has ordered us to stand down," an angel of the flock said, tilting his head strangely to one side as he addressed his brethren. "It is not our place to question."

"It is not our place to sit and allow the offenders of His will to go unpunished," another replied.

They all ruffled the feathers of their wings menacingly. Dissension was brewing in the ranks of the Powers, the likes of which Kraus had never perceived. *Is this the reason I feel such dread?* he wondered. *Or is there something more?* He thought of the enigmatic Archons and the mysterious prisoner they still held in the abandoned St. Athanasius Orphanage.

Then a shudder passed through the healer as he recalled the moment his new eyes first beheld their master—his master. Kraus felt ashamed, for here was the being that had given his miserable life purpose, given him the gift of sight, and rather than feeling love and gratitude, he experienced only an inexplicable revulsion and fear.

There came a disturbance in the sky above the rooftop, and Kraus watched in wonder as the air began to shimmer like water, growing increasingly darker as Verchiel appeared. The angel leader touched down upon the tar roof, opening his expansive wings to reveal the blind Archon, Katspiel, huddled within their folds. The magick user was bent over, his body twisted with fatigue. Kraus could hear him gasping for air, fluid rattling in his lungs. He was about to go to the Archon, to see if he could help, when Verchiel began to address what remained of his army.

"Rally yourselves, my brethren," their leader proclaimed, "for I have need of your warrior skills!"

The roosting angels spread their wings and leaped into the air to circle about their master, agitated cries of anticipation issuing from their mouths. The Archon raised his arm, a tremulous hand weaving the fabric of a magickal spell in the air, coalescing like drifting cobwebs to affix to their bodies.

"The last two Malakim have been found," Verchiel bellowed as the air around them began to distort. "The final fragments of the rite we seek will soon be in our grasp."

"Know as I know," Katspiel pronounced, still casting his spell. "See as I see."

One by one the angels nodded, knowing where they must go to obtain their master's prize. With nary a question, they wrapped themselves in their wings and were gone. Verchiel was the last to depart, closing his eyes and smiling as his feathered appendages slowly closed about him and the Archon.

"Closer and closer still," he said, his voice tainted with the thrill of anticipation, and then they, too, were gone.

The sense of foreboding was with Kraus again, stronger than any of the others, and a small part of him longed for the way things used to be, before he was given sight and truly began to see.

Things seemed so much clearer then.

Aaron sat on the cluttered floor and thumbed through a book of art. The book depicted various interpretations of Heaven and Hell by artists with names like Blake, Doré, and Bosch. He was paying close attention to the artists' renditions of Hell.

"So let me see if I understand this," he said, looking up from a particularly disturbing take on the underworld that showed the damned being mauled by demons and eaten by mutant animals in a landscape of mind-boggling chaos, painted by the Dutch artist Hieronymus Bosch. "According to you, there is no Hell."

Scholar was in the process of preparing himself

yet another cup of tea. Aaron had noticed the many small tables set up throughout the expansive library so the fallen angel could enjoy his hot beverage wherever he happened to be working.

"Let's try this again, shall we? Hell is not a place, per se," the angel said, removing the dripping bag from his cup and dropping it onto a plate on the table. "It is more a state of being— an experience, if you will."

Aaron closed the heavy volume and climbed to his feet to return the book to its shelf. "But there is a Heaven?" he asked, just to be certain.

Scholar intercepted him before he could reach the bookcase, probably worried that the boy would put it back in the wrong place or maybe topple the bookcases. "Of course there is a Heaven," he answered sharply, exasperated that Aaron could even ask such a question. "Otherwise the whole reason for your conception wouldn't even exist." He pointedly returned the art text to its proper place.

Aaron shrugged, leaning back casually against one of the packed shelves. "I thought that one couldn't exist without the other."

Scholar returned to his steaming brew, picking up the mug to drink. "Humankind has been fascinated by the concept of an underworld, a Hell, since first leaving the trees—sitting around blazing campfires, speculating about the fate of their souls after death." He took a sip and closed his eyes, the warm fluid passing over his lips, seeming to bring the high-strung angel a certain amount of calm.

"They wondered what would happen when they were no more, struggling to unravel the vast mysteries of life in a strange and unknowable world. The early humans wove all manner of fantastic tales about underworld deities and perilous journeys to the afterlife. The stories were passed from parent to child by word of mouth, with every generation adding a little of its own spice to the mix. Organized religion fine-tuned these theories into elaborate cause-and-effect scenarios, but it always meant the same: good behavior meant salvation; evil, damnation."

"So if Hell isn't a place, what is it really?" Aaron asked.

Scholar chuckled, but there was no amusement in his response as he stared off into space. "If you asked each of us who has fallen, you would likely receive a different answer from each," he said. "To some, being banished from Heaven was the ultimate damnation." The angel paused and caught Aaron's eye before continuing. "But it was your sire, the son of the morning—Lucifer Morningstar—that experienced, and probably still endures, a level of Hell in which all others pale in comparison."

"It was his punishment," Aaron stated firmly, "for what he did to Heaven."

Scholar nodded slowly, and Aaron knew he

was reliving the moment God bestowed His punishment upon the angel that was his own father. "All the pain, all the violence that he was responsible for, was collected in one seething mass of misery." The angel's face twisted. He held up his empty hand as if clutching a ball of something terrible. "And it was put inside him so that he would forever feel the extent of the suffering he caused." Scholar touched his chest, acting out Lucifer's fate. "He was the first of the fallen, and those who had taken up his cause followed him to Earth, sharing in his banishment from Heaven."

"Where did he go?" Aaron asked. *If there is no Hell, where does the Devil live?* he wondered, recalling some neighborhoods in his hometown of Lynn that the Devil would have been quite comfortable in.

"Lucifer wandered the globe. Some say he was so bitterly angry with God that he turned to evil, doing everything in his power to corrupt the world of which the Creator was so proud." Scholar finished what could have been his tenth cup of tea since Aaron arrived and set the used cup down on a tabletop.

"And what do you think?" Aaron asked. "Was he evil or was that just a bad rap that followed him because of what he did in Heaven?"

"If he was a creature of evil," Scholar began thoughtfully. "If he was the unrepenting scourge that your popular culture suggests, would it have been possible for him to conceive a being whose sole reason for living is to bring redemption not only for himself, but for all who were tempted by him? I think not."

"I can see why Verchiel and his Powers aren't so thrilled with me," Aaron said as things began to tumble into place in his mind. "If everything goes according to the prophecy, I'll be responsible for granting forgiveness to the ultimate sinner, one that Verchiel feels should suffer for his crimes for all eternity."

Scholar nodded in agreement. "Verchiel still believes in his mission, no matter how foul and twisted it has become. He still believes in the ultimate punishment for those who questioned the Word of God."

The enormity of his responsibility to the fallen angels, to his father, to God Himself, landed upon Aaron's shoulders like a ton of bricks. He was finally getting used to the idea of reuniting the fallen with God, but to repair a rift between God and the Devil? That was another thing entirely.

"Do you think he deserves to be forgiven?" Aaron asked Scholar.

The fallen angel smiled sadly and shrugged his shoulders. "That's not for me to decide."

"But if it *was*," Aaron persisted.

"Then yes, I would forgive him," Scholar said. "If we pathetic creatures can receive absolution, then so should he, for he did only what the others of us were not brave or strong enough to do ourselves."

Aaron thought for a moment. "Guess I'm going to have to find this Lucifer and see for myself," he said with a hint of a smile. "But not before I deal with a certain Powers commander."

He was about to ask Scholar if they had learned anything more about Verchiel's whereabouts, when from somewhere far off in the room he heard a door thrown violently open and his name being called. Aaron recognized the sound of Lehash's voice as well as the intensity in it and hurried to find Aerie's head of security, with a curious Scholar close behind.

Aaron ran around the corner of a wall of bookcases and nearly head-on into the gunslinger. "What's wrong?" he gasped, not liking the look he saw in Lehash's eyes.

"There's trouble at the house," the angel began. "It's Vilma, she . . ."

Aaron didn't wait for him to finish. Immediately the image of the home in which the girl he loved was staying formed in his mind. His wings of solid black surged from his back, toppling stacks of books as they closed around him, Scholar's frantic gasps the last sound heard before he was gone in the blink of an eye.

chapter six

Traversing the void between the here and there, Verchiel listened to the fearsome shrieks of his soldiers. They sensed the battle to come, and reveled in the opportunity to honor him; their cries of war an inspiration to his cause.

Verchiel had never trusted the Malakim. He had always been suspicious of the level of knowledge and power that had been conferred on the angelic trinity by the Supreme Being. How ironic that these same gifts would be used against their most Holy Father. It almost amused him, but since the horrible realization that he had been cast adrift by the same Master he had most dutifully served since the beginning of time, there was very little room left for amusement.

They were close now; Verchiel could feel their presence, their complex magicks no longer able to hide them. The Archon Katspiel had again proven his worth. Though it drained his life force like a thirsty desert nomad sucking greedily upon a canteen, the angelic magick user had managed to weave an intricate spell that revealed the secret location of the two surviving Malakim.

What's that monkey expression I've heard so many times? Verchiel mused. *Two birds with a single rock,* he thought as his wings parted to reveal his journey's end.

Two Malakim, clothed in shimmering robes seemingly woven from the purest sunlight, stood over the body of the first of their kind slain at Kilimanjaro. His armored body had been laid out upon an ancient stone altar and encircled with burning candles of various heights. The inscrutable creatures of Heaven, oft believed to be as close to God as any of His creations, were mourning their kindred's passing. *How quaintly . . . human,* Verchiel thought while he surveyed their whereabouts.

They had traveled to a vast cave, its walls dappled with man-size recesses filled with desiccated remains. The stink of the dead hung heavy in the stagnant air. Based upon the religious trappings around the cavern, Verchiel gathered that they were in some early Christian burial chamber, long forgotten and probably hidden deep beneath some sprawling metropolis. The Malakim had always been fascinated with the ways of the human monkeys, observing their every movement along the evolutionary path. Verchiel still believed the species to be little more than clever animals and saw no real future for them. And if he accomplished what he'd set out to do, there would indeed be none.

"You have not been bidden here, angel," one of the Malakim said, his voice dripping with conceit. "Take your host and depart. We respect your empathy, but wish to grieve for our departed brother alone."

Was that the slightest hint of fear Verchiel saw on the faces of these supposedly superior beings as they stood over the remains of their brother? How disturbing it must have been for them, to find one of their own brought down to ground, its most precious resource torn from its body.

"We didn't wish it to be this way," he said to the Malakim, moving closer. He noticed that they had cleaned the corpse, but it did little to hide the ravages of the Powers' search for their prize. "We begged him to surrender, but he chose instead to fight."

The two angelic beings shared a quick glance before looking back to Verchiel. It was exactly as it had been with the first of their ilk: so arrogant that they couldn't even begin to fathom the idea that they would soon be under siege.

"It was as if he wanted to die," Verchiel said, gazing down upon the corpse in mock sadness and then smiling a predator's smile.

At that moment, the Malakim finally understood, and the look upon their oh-so-superior faces was priceless. The Powers leader raised his hand. "Take them," he barked to his troops.

His warriors sprang at his command, weapons of flame appearing for battle. Startled by this overt display of hostility, the Malakim backed away from the stone altar on which their fallen comrade had been laid.

"The others have arrived," Archon Katspiel whispered, his sightless head tilted back, nose twitching, and Verchiel saw that he was correct. The air behind the distracted Malakim had begun to distort, a magickal entrance for the remaining Archons.

The Malakim were standing back to back, the blessed light of their divinity radiating from their bodies, illuminating the ugliness of the burial chamber around them, the heat thrown from their omnipotence igniting the remains of the interred. Weapons of crackling, blue force had appeared in their hands, and they fought Verchiel's soldiers with a ferocity that impressed the Powers leader greatly. If only they would give up their knowledge willingly and join him in his endeavor against a Creator that had gone mad. But Verchiel knew that it would never come to be, for he imagined they were still under the misconception that their God could do no wrong, and nothing would sway them from their faith.

Poor deluded fools.

His Powers did what was expected of them, their fury relentless, their numbers expendable for the greater good. Many had begun to burn, the intense heat radiating from the Malakim devouring their flesh with a ravenous hunger, but still they fought, the first wave of a two pronged assault.

The Archons had taken up their positions behind the battle, their arms waving in the air as they recited incantations that would render their prey helpless. From Verchiel's side, Katspiel joined his voice to his fellow magicians as he removed the sacred blade of extraction from within the folds of his robe.

A high-pitched squeal echoed through the burial chamber, and one of the Malakim fell, writhing and twitching upon the mausoleum floor, fighting the Archon's magick. But the other acted as his partner fell, conjuring a shield, a protective bubble that kept out the spell of incapacitation, as well as the fury of the remaining Powers soldiers.

Verchiel spread his wings and leaped into the air, a sword coming to life in his grasp. "Step aside," he bellowed as he landed before the crackling sphere of magickal energy that contained his quarry. His surviving warriors, blackened and blistered, quickly scattered.

"Give me what I want, and I will let you live," Verchiel said as he placed his hand against the sphere. There was a flash of supernatural energies and the Powers commander pulled quickly away, his palm blackened by the discharge.

"We know what you took from brother Peliel," the Malakim said from within the bubble. He had fallen to his knees, exhausted from the expenditure. "You tamper with forces far beyond your capacity to understand. I ask you, angel of the Powers host, to abandon this madness before it is too late."

Verchiel smiled, more snarl then grin, and ran his tongue over the tender flesh of his burned palm. He turned away from the sphere to look upon the Archon Katspiel. The blind sorcerer had found his way across the room and now stood over the body of the Malakim they had brought down, clutching the fearsome tool of extraction.

"Katspiel," Verchiel said, looking back to the magickally protected Malakim. "Take what I came for."

The blind Archon raised his arm, preparing to bring the dagger down.

"Please," the divine being begged from within his sphere of protective energy. "Allow us our lives and we'll give you what you want."

"Raphael, no!" shrieked the Malakim beneath the awful dagger, eyes wide in defiance.

"Silence!" Verchiel ordered, turning his attentions back to the Malakim Raphael. "Drop the spell of protection and I will consider your offer."

Raphael stared at the Powers commander for a moment, then did as he was ordered, the bubble of magickal energy dissipating in the air, like the smoke from the burning remains within the burial chamber. "It is done," he said.

"Yes. Yes, it is," Verchiel replied. "Katspiel."

The Archon brought the dagger down into the skull of the immobilized Malakim, the sound of splitting skull explosive in the quiet air of the tomb.

"Your offer is too costly," Verchiel said to the surviving Malakim. "You and your brother are too dangerous to be left alive. I hope you can understand my position."

The angelic being nodded as the Archons surrounded him, the spell of immobilization beginning to spill from their lips. "As I hope you will understand mine," Raphael said. A sword of crackling energy sprang suddenly to life in his grasp and he spun around to plunge it into the chest of the nearest angelic magician.

Chaos erupted. The Archons began to scream, their concentration broken as Jaldabaoth slumped to the ground, the blade of light protruding from his chest. The surviving Powers soldiers surged forward in an attempt to apprehend the last of the Malakim. But Verchiel already knew it was too late. Raphael had taken advantage of the moment, and before they could put their hands upon him or recast their spells, he had sprouted wings of gold and taken flight.

Aaron felt the ground appear beneath his feet and opened his wings, his blood running cold with the sight before him. The girl he loved was attacking Lorelei and Gabriel. *No, not the girl I love,* he corrected himself, *but the ancient power that has spun out of control within her.*

Vilma was screaming, an ear-piercing mixture of anger and pain, as supernatural flame streamed from her fingertips to consume everything it touched. Lorelei had extended her arm, and a spell of defense spilled from her mouth as she attempted to restrain the rampant Nephilim. Tendrils of magickal force erupted from her outstretched hand, striking Vilma and knocking her violently to the ground. Aaron was moving to help her when the girl began to shriek—a scream he had heard before. A scream he himself had bellowed in times of battle. It was a cry of war.

Aaron opened his mouth to warn Lorelei of the impending danger, but it was too late. The flash was blinding, an explosion of heavenly fire that propelled the Nephilim sorceress backward, her body landing in a broken heap in the front yard. Vilma was on her feet again and she began to wander toward the street, but Gabriel surged forward to block her path.

"C'mon, Vilma," he said to her. "*You've got to calm down before somebody really gets hurt.*"

And Aaron noticed then that his dog was burned, patches of Gabriel's beautiful, golden yellow coat still smoldering from the bite of the angelic essence. He held his breath, watching as the girl gazed at the canine obstacle, her head tilting strangely to one side, the angelic essence peering out through her eyes.

"That's it," the dog continued in a soothing, rumble of a voice. *"No need to be so upset, we can work it out."*

They were still unaware of his presence and Aaron remained perfectly still; at the moment Gabriel seemed to have the situation under control and he didn't want to disturb a thing if this had a chance of working. Since his rebirth, the dog had developed a number of rather unique abilities. It seemed that there was a strange psychic connection between the Labrador and all things Nephilim. If there was anybody that could calm the raging angelic essence, it was Gabriel.

"I'm . . . I'm trying," Vilma said, her voice small and trembling. She sounded very far away. "But it's fighting me."

Aaron saw the tears streaming down her face and his heart just about broke. He remembered how painful it had been for him when he had tried to hold back his own emerging angelic essence.

"I'll help you," Gabriel said. *"Just let me inside your thoughts and we'll see if we can't put it back to sleep. That's it,"* the dog cooed.

The girl began to sway slowly, her eyes clamped tightly shut. Gabriel swayed as well, psychically connected, adding his own strength to hers. But suddenly her body stiffened and a gasp of agony escaped her lips. Gabriel yelped as well, recoiling from the psychic pain. And then Aaron heard the sound of something tearing.

"Gabriel, get away from her!" he screamed in warning, waving his arms as he ran toward them, his sneakered feet slipping on the wet grass, the smell of things burning assailing his nostrils.

Vilma cried out as the wings, hidden beneath the flesh of her back, began to grow. Her clothing tore as they slowly unfurled. If the moment hadn't been so intense, Aaron would have thought them the most beautiful wings he had ever seen; fawn feathers, dappled with spots of white, brown and black.

Her body shuddered with release, her new wings fanning the air. She gazed down upon Gabriel, a sneer of cruelty on her tear-stained face. The dog seemed stunned as he sat before the out of control Nephilim, furiously shaking his head.

The language of messengers—the language of angels—poured from Vilma's mouth. She extended her arms toward the helpless Lab and heavenly fire began to dance at her fingertips.

Aaron pushed his wings from his back and leaped the final few feet to his best friend. The flame cascaded off his back, over his wings of glistening black, and he cried out as he pulled Gabriel into his protective embrace.

"You're going to run now," he whispered into the dog's ear through gritted teeth as the fire lapped at his back.

Gabriel seemed to gather his wits about him, and he sprinted from his master's arms to safety behind a nearby tree.

Aaron whirled around, the stench of burning flesh and feathers choking the air. He sprang from the ground, propelling himself toward Vilma, his shoulder connecting with her midsection. He didn't want to hurt her, but she had to be stopped. The power inside her, if left unchecked, would threaten not only Aerie, but the human world outside as well.

He drove her backward into the front of the house. The force of their strike shattering the window above their heads.

"Listen to me, Vilma," he said, tryng to pin her flailing arms against the house. "Listen to the sound of my voice."

She cried out a shrill, birdlike shriek as she thrashed from side to side.

"You're stronger than this," he continued, trying to keep his voice calm, even though the burns on his back throbbed with his every movement. "You have to force it down where it belongs. It's not stronger than you; it just wants you to think it is."

She stopped struggling, her body growing slack, and Aaron mistakenly loosened his hold upon her. Still firmly in the grip of the angelic power, Vilma drove her knee up into his groin and he fell to the ground gasping for air.

She continued to rant and rave in the tongue of angels as she slowly beat the air with her wings, preparing for her first flight. One word stuck out from all the rest.

"Escape!"

But that was something Aaron couldn't allow. Through the haze of pain, he tried to straighten his body enough to grab at her—to keep her on the ground—but his fingers only brushed the hem of her jeans as she took to the air. And then a yellow blur moved past him, latching onto Vilma's leg with a furious grip. Gabriel growled as Vilma kicked at him, but he held firm, giving Aaron enough time to gather his wits and take to the air.

He managed to grab hold of the girl, but she beat her wings furiously and still they climbed higher. Gabriel released his hold on her, falling harmlessly to the ground, where he stood staring up at them, locked in a struggle above the rooftop.

Fire again shot from her outstretched hands, knocking Aaron away with its scouring blast. She was flying away from him now, frantically trying to flee, and he realized there was only one thing he could do to stop her. He summoned a sword of fire, watching as its deadly shape took form in his grasp. Then he poured on the speed cutting through the air, like a hungry shark zeroing in upon its hapless prey. *This is the only way,* he repeated in his mind as he flew above her and lashed out with his weapon, cutting into one of her beautiful new wings.

Her scream was piercing as she floundered in the air attempting to stay aloft, but the pain was too great, the injury too extensive, and Vilma began to fall from the sky. Aaron wished his sword away and dived to catch her flailing body. "Let me help," he pleaded.

But the essence roared its ire, flames exploding from her hands and driving him away. Helplessly, he followed her path of descent, watching as she landed on the street below, scattering a crowd of citizens who had gathered to watch the battle.

He crouched beside her and took her into his arms. She was alive but seemed to be in the grip of nightmare, moaning and thrashing in his embrace. It was only a matter of time before she regained consciousness and he didn't know what to do.

"You might want to step away from her," he heard Lehash say from somewhere close by, and turned to see the angel aiming one of his golden weapons, hammer already cocked. "It's probably the most merciful thing to do."

Aaron pulled her closer, shielding her from

harm. "You want to kill her?" he cried incredulously. "Are you out of your mind? Is that how you solve problems here, by putting bullets in them?"

Lehash lowered his weapon with a heavy sigh and stepped closer. "You know that's not what I'm about, boy," he said quietly. "The merger's just not happening right with her. She's a danger to herself—to us and the world." The gunslinger angel gripped Aaron's shoulder and squeezed. "Puttin' her down might just be the best thing for her."

"I can't let you do that," the boy said, looking from Lehash to Vilma. "I have to try and help her."

The gun in Lehash's hand disappeared in a flash of light, but Aaron knew it could be back in an instant. "And what if you can't? What if this is one that can't be saved?"

Aaron didn't answer the fallen angel. Instead he pulled the girl even closer, whispering softly in her ear that everything was going to be all right, and wishing with all his might for it to be true.

Deep within the realm of unconsciousness, Lucifer fled into a place of his own creation to escape the agonies of torture.

He lay upon the bed beside her, knowing full well that she was but a figment from his past, a creation of his pain-addled mind. But he could not help but feel a spike of joy having Taylor beside him again.

"What?" she asked, looking into his eyes. "Is there something wrong?"

Where to begin? Lucifer pondered. He considered wishing it all away, to return to the darkness of oblivion, to the bleak reality of his situation, but he couldn't bring himself to do so.

"No," he finally said, feeling somewhat guilty for the lie, even though she was only a creation of his mind. "Everything's fine. Why don't you go back to sleep?"

Taylor sat up in bed, the strap of her nightgown sliding off her shoulder to expose the curves of her delicate flesh. "You're not a very good liar, you know that?" she said with a knowing smile. "Maybe if we talk about it, you'll feel better, come up with something that you didn't think of before."

He found it strangely amusing that he tried to lie to an invention of his own imagination, as if it wouldn't already be aware of the danger he was in.

Lucifer rolled away and climbed from the bed. "There's really nothing to talk about." His environment suddenly changed, like a scene-shift in a motion picture, the quiet darkness of the bedroom blurring into a park on a beautiful summer's day.

"Try me," Taylor said, her hand firmly clasped in his.

Her silk nightgown had been replaced with a simple sundress, sandals, and a floppy, wide-brimmed hat. It was the outfit she had been wearing when they'd first met so long ago. A dog, a golden retriever that he already knew was named Brandy, bounded toward them, a stick in its mouth, eager for a game of fetch.

It was an absolutely beautiful day, just as he remembered. The sky was bluer than he had ever seen it, wispy clouds like spider's silk stretching across the broad turquoise expanse. It was a day unlike any other he had spent upon the world of his banishment—the day when he first considered that he could be something *more* than the first of the fallen, the monster that had brought about a war in Paradise.

How foolish he had been.

Taylor took the stick from the dog and threw it. "Do you think he'll actually do it?" she asked, watching the dog bound across the green, green grass in pursuit of its prize.

She was speaking about Verchiel and the angel's intention to use Lucifer as an instrument of death to strike at the heart of the Creator—by destroying His world. He would have liked to believe that nothing that sprang from the loins of God could do such evil, but he had looked into the eyes of the Powers commander and saw something angry and twisted—something familiar—and he knew the answer.

"Yes, I think he will," Lucifer said.

Brandy returned happily with the stick, and he noticed that the sky had grown suddenly darker, as if there were a storm brewing. This had not been part of their original day and Lucifer grew wary.

"And do you think he'll succeed?" the woman asked, squatting down to pat the dog, running her nails through its long, golden brown fur and rubbing its ears.

The sky had turned the color of night and thunder rumbled ominously in the distance. "In order for Verchiel to destroy the world of man, he must somehow undo the Word of God," Lucifer replied as the darkness closed in around them. "And I doubt that even one as tenacious as he can concoct a way in which to do that."

The rain began to fall in drenching torrents, and he took her by the hand and pulled her to her feet, and they ran for cover. Brandy had already deserted them, fleeing into the permanent midnight that had consumed all evidence of the park.

He put his arm around Taylor, holding her close to him, fearing that he might lose her in the storm. She was soaked, and he felt her tremble as they stumbled through the dreamscape in search of shelter.

A cave was suddenly before them, like the open maw of the great whale ready to swallow Jonah, and as they approached, a feeling of unease swept over him and he recoiled.

"What's the matter?" Taylor asked, pushing her wet hair away from her face. "Do you know this place?" And he knew full well that she knew he did.

"It's not a place I care to visit," he said, staring into the Cimmerian space beyond the cave's entrance.

Taylor tugged at his hand, pulling him toward the cave. "We should go inside," she suggested. "Just for a little while, to get out of the rain."

Every instinct screamed for him to run, but he allowed himself to be pulled along, and the darkness enveloped them in an embrace that chilled him to his very core.

Torches came to life as they walked deeper into the cave. There were crude drawings upon the walls depicting God's creation of the universe, of the beings that He would call His angels. He saw himself sitting at the Creator's right hand as the Earth formed beneath them.

"That really pissed you off, didn't it?" Taylor asked. The passage in which they walked angled steeply downward.

"Yes, it did," Lucifer admitted, eyeing the interpretation of Eden and its first human residents. He still felt the fury as if for the first time. "I was jealous of them. I thought that He was pushing us aside for the humans—that He loved them more than us."

They continued their descent, the passage

opening wider, the paintings now dwarfing them with their size.

"Did you have to start a war?" She gave his hand a loving squeeze. "Couldn't you have just had a nice talk? Told Him how you were feeling?"

The pictures showed Lucifer gathering his army and giving them a gift of his inner strength.

"I was angry."

"No kidding," Taylor said, pointing out a particularly fearsome depiction of himself, flaming sword in hand as he led his troops into battle against the forces of Heaven.

The wall art that followed was of things that he didn't care to see. Paintings of his army's defeat, of the deaths of those that had sworn him allegiance, the survivors fleeing Heaven to hide upon the earth.

"I bet seeing it drawn out like this makes you feel pretty stupid," Taylor said with a sigh.

"You don't know the half of it," Lucifer answered. "But somehow you learn to live with and accept the mistakes that you made."

They had reached the end of the passage, the final drawing before them an image of himself, broken, beaten, skin blackened and charred, as the hand of God came down from the heavens to deliver His verdict upon him.

"And His punishment?" she asked, unconsciously rubbing her own chest at the point where God had touched him—where all the pain and sorrow that he had caused was placed. "Have you accepted that?"

Lucifer slowly nodded, his eyes riveted to the artistic representation of his fate. "It is what I deserved," he said, reaching out to place the palm of his hand upon the cool stone wall that marked the end of their journey.

And as his hand came in contact with the wall, a shudder went through the painted rock. Large cracks appeared, splitting the stone. Lucifer was quick to act, gripping Taylor by the arm and pulling her from the path of harm as the stone wall before them fell away to reveal something hidden behind it.

They stared in awe as the dust began to settle, and they looked upon an enormous door of metal. It reminded him of a bank vault, only far larger, its surface crisscrossed with thick chains and fortified with multiple locks of every imaginable size.

Instinctively he knew what he was looking at—what *they* were looking at—and was in awe of it. Here was the psychic representation of God's Word, the curse that kept the accumulated pain and sorrow of the War in Heaven locked away inside of him.

"And Verchiel would have to get through *that* to achieve his plans?" Taylor asked, pointing to the enormous door.

Lucifer was about to respond, to reassure her that nothing short of God Himself could access the obstacle that kept his hellish penance at bay, when he felt a tremor pass through the tunnel, and the great door rattled in its frame of ancient rock. They both watched in growing horror as a padlock connecting two links of a mighty chain sprang open, clattering to floor.

"That's exactly what he would have to do," Lucifer said, an icy claw of dread closing upon his heart as another of the locks fell away.

chapter seven

Aaron stifled a cry of discomfort as Lorelei dabbed some salve on the wounds he sustained during his altercation with Vilma. It smelled absolutely horrible and stung even worse. But she had already chastised him once about being a baby, embarrassing him in front of Lehash, so he gritted his teeth and endured the pain.

"Are you almost done back there?" he asked.

"Just about," she said as he felt her attach a dampened bandage to his shoulder. "That oughta take care of that." She gently pressed the bandage against his burned skin. It felt cool—almost soothing—but then the throbbing was back.

"Until she loses it again," Lehash added, pulling one of his foul-smelling cheroots from his duster pocket.

"That's not the least bit funny." Aaron glared at the angel.

"It wasn't meant to be, boy," the gunslinger said, lifting his index finger to the tip of the thin cigar in his mouth.

"Don't you dare light that filthy thing in here," Scholar bellowed from across the room. "The books will stink of it for months." The angel was sitting at a small wooden desk, his back to them, as he continued to peruse the books he had gathered, hoping to find a solution to Vilma's problem.

"And you wonder why I don't visit," Lehash grumbled, taking the cigar from his mouth and returning it to his pocket.

The mood was depressingly grim. Neither Lorelei nor Lehash held out much hope for Vilma, but Aaron wasn't about to give up that easily. If anyone in Aerie could help her, it was Scholar.

The fallen angel threw up his hands in exasperation and rose from his seat. "I've found nothing," he said, beginning to pace. "There's plenty about Nephilim, but nothing on how to control them once they're out of balance."

Lehash leaned back against a bookcase and crossed his arms. "And you know why that is?" he asked. "Because there *isn't* any way, and that's one of the reasons why the Powers started killing Nephilim. The angelic essence is sometimes too much for the human aspect to deal with; it's too strong and it takes control—makes 'em crazy, dangerous."

"She's not crazy *or* dangerous," Aaron grumbled, slipping on a fresh shirt.

"Right now she ain't, and that's only because we got her knocked out with one of Lorelei's special potions, and wearing a pair'a them magickal bracelets. Hell, we even got that dog of yours over there trying to keep her from getting her feathers ruffled."

Aaron's thoughts raced. He didn't like where this was going. There had to be something they could do to help her. "What about the ritual I went through with Belphegor?" he asked. "Wasn't that to help my two natures unify properly? Why couldn't we do that with—"

Scholar shook his head. "She'd never survive it. The angelic nature is already stronger than her human half. It would eat her alive and we'd have the same problem we started with: pure angelic power running amok."

"And we can't have that, Aaron," Lehash said grimly. "It may not be what you want, but somethin's got to be done before she gets outta hand again."

Aaron shook his head. They'd already given up on her. "I'm not hearing this," he said, turning to face them all. Lorelei wouldn't make eye contact, arranging her bottles and vials of healing remedies in a pink, plastic makeup case. "I refuse to believe that there's nothing we can do for Vilma, short of putting her down like some sick animal."

They said nothing, refusing to provide him with even the slightest glimmer of hope.

"Lorelei," Aaron said, watching as she visibly flinched, "with your angel magick, there's nothing you can do that might help?"

She shook her head, finally meeting his gaze. "You're talking about binding a divine essence. I haven't the training or the knowledge to—"

Aaron suddenly clapped his hands and whirled toward Scholar. "The knowledge," he repeated moving toward the angel. "Lorelei doesn't have the knowledge, but maybe somebody else does." He stopped short before the scholarly angel. "Who would have more knowledge than Lorelei? How did she learn what she knows? Who taught the magick user?"

Scholar shrugged his shoulders and tugged at his ear nervously. "Belphegor taught her quite a bit, and then there are books and scrolls. But Vilma's problem, like I already told you, isn't addressed in—"

"Who taught Belphegor?" Aaron persisted. "Who wrote the books and the scrolls?" He gestured to them for help. "C'mon guys, give me something—anything."

"Most of what we have comes from the Archons," Scholar said slowly.

"But what's left of them hooked up with Verchiel and his Powers," Lehash said stepping away from the bookcase.

Aaron felt his anger flare and struggled to

prevent his wings from bursting forth and the sigils from rising upon his flesh. "Damn it," he swore beneath his breath, feeling his own ray of hope beginning to dim.

"Who taught the Archons?" Lorelei said softly and they all looked at her, although Scholar and Lehash remained strangely silent.

"Well?" Aaron prodded. "The lady asked a question. Who taught the Archons?"

Scholar turned back to his books. "It's too much of a long shot," he said, stacking the texts. "I wouldn't want you to get your hopes up."

"Too late," Aaron said walking to Scholar and gripping his arm. "Who are they?"

"You're clutching at straws here, boy," Lehash echoed. "We don't have the time to be wastin' on—"

Aaron whirled to glare at the gunslinger, this time letting the sigils of warriors that died serving the will of Lucifer appear on his flesh. "I don't want to hear that," he growled, and watched as Lehash backed down, averting his eyes.

"Who taught the Archons?" he asked Scholar firmly, and there would be no debate.

"They're called the Malakim," Scholar replied, an air of reverence in his tone. "And if you can't get a meeting with the Lord God Almighty, then they're the next best thing.

Do we truly understand what we are doing? Archon Oraios wondered as he lifted the lid of the golden chest containing the paraphernalia of their mystical art. *Or have we been blinded by the obsession of the one that commands us—drawn into the web of his madness, no longer able to escape?*

"Where is the dirt?" Archon Jao screeched, crouching within the circle of containment beneath Lucifer's hanging body. The angel frantically checked and rechecked the metal clamps affixed to the first of the fallen's chest to keep his incision pulled wide and taut. The bleeding had stopped sometime ago, and now the hint of a pulsing, red glow could be seen leaking from the splayed chest cavity. "I must have the dirt," Jao demanded.

Archon Oraios continued to search. The bag of sacred earth was crucial to their preparations. It was soil from the fields of Heaven, a powerful component of angelic sorceries, used to fortify and maintain the strength of more dangerous magicks. A small, frightened part of him hoped to never find it, forcing them to abandon this dangerous and blasphemous ritual.

But alas, there it was—in a place he had already checked twice. *Is a higher mystical force attempting to intervene, to prevent them from making a horrible mistake?* he pondered.

"Did you find it?" Archon Domiel prodded, tension filling his voice.

With the death of their brother Jaldabaoth at the hands of the Malakim Raphael, their numbers were fewer, and all were feeling the strain.

Only one more Malakim remained, one final shard of forbidden information, and then they would do the unthinkable: reverse the Word of God. And a plague of despair, the likes of which the world had never known, would wash over the land.

"Here," Oraios said, pulling from the chest the purse, made from the skin of an animal that had thrived in the garden before the death of the Eden.

"Quickly now," Jao insisted, his outstretched hand beckoning for the precious, magickal component.

Oraios handed the pouch to his brother and watched as Jao carefully spilled a portion of the rich, black contents into his open palm. The scent of Heaven wafted through the stale air of the abandoned school, and Oraios found himself transported back to Paradise by the memories stored within the fragrant aroma of the blessed earth.

He'd always believed that he would return there someday, to again witness the towering crystal spires reaching up into forever, the endless fields of golden grass, whispering softly, caressed by the gentle winds, and to bask again in the radiance of His glory.

But then Oraios returned to reality and gazed upon the form of the Morningstar, suspended with chains above a mystic circle drawn in his lifeblood and fortified with the dirt of providence. The Archon felt his dreams sadly slip away, resigning himself to his fate.

"It is only a matter of time now," he mused aloud, watching as his brothers continued their preparations, the images of Heaven in his mind already starting to fade.

"I don't think you understand what I'm trying to say," Scholar said to the savior of Aerie, dipping his tea bag again and again in the steaming cup of water just poured from the electric teapot. "Malakim are mysteries even to us."

"So they're a mystery, fine. I'm cool with that," Aaron said, a twinkle of optimism in his eyes. "All I need to know is if they can help Vilma."

Scholar sipped his drink without removing the bag. A good, strong brew was required for *this* conversation. "Yes, I would imagine. If there are any beings of an angelic nature out there that might have the knowledge to solve Ms. Santiago's problem, it would be they, but—"

"No 'buts,'" Aaron said with a quick shake of his head. "This is the closest we've come to a solution and I'm not about to lose it."

"But it isn't close enough," Lehash said. Aerie's constable had helped himself to a cup of coffee and a seat, leaning the chair back on two legs against the wall. Ignoring Scholar's looks of disapproval, he continued. "The Malakim have become legends to us—like Merlin or Paul

Bunyan and his blue ox to the humans."

Aaron closed his eyes and took in a deep breath. "So are they real or are they made up?"

The gunslinger slurped the remainder of his coffee and brought the front legs of his chair down upon the floor with a thud. "There might be some truth in all the tall tales, but it's been jumbled together over the years, and it's hard to tell fact from fiction."

Lorelei spoke up from a workstation tabletop where she sat cross-legged, reading through an ancient text where the Malakim were briefly mentioned. "It says here that they were the arch mages of angelic magick and keepers of forbidden knowledge." She flipped her snow-white hair back over her shoulder and out of her face. "Knowledge known only to God."

"What we do know for certain," Scholar continued, "is that the Malakim were created to be extensions of God, the receptacles of all His wisdom and knowledge—forbidden or otherwise."

"It's that knowledge thing I'm interested in," Aaron said. "Where can we find these Malakim?" he asked. "Do you know—"

"The Malakim supposedly came to Earth after the war in Heaven," Scholar interrupted. "To study and record the changes caused by the fallen."

"How can they be contacted?" Aaron asked, his patience clearly wearing thin.

Scholar set his mug down, immediately craving another cup. "That's what I've been trying to tell you, Aaron. The Malakim have hidden themselves away. There hasn't been any contact between our kind and them for thousands upon thousands of years."

"I can't believe this," the Nephilim said, sitting down on the bare floor and running his fingers through his hair. His voice was heavy with disappointment. "Have you ever actually seen one?" he finally asked, looking up at Scholar.

"No, but—"

"Have *any* of you seen one?" Aaron prodded climbing to his feet.

"Well, it might have been a Malakim," Lehash began, rubbing his stubble-covered chin. "But I can't say for sure."

Scholar quickly turned and walked to farthest end of the room. Aaron wanted proof of the existence of the Malakim, and proof he would have. It was kept in a glass case along with all the other treasures of Aerie. He carefully opened the lid and removed the ornate cylinder from its resting place upon a red velvet pillow.

They were all staring as he returned, still startled by his abrupt departure. He held the canister up for Aaron to see.

"You want to know how we are sure the Malakim exist?" he asked, heading for the workstation where Lorelei sat. She hopped down as he approached. "Belphegor gave this to me for safe-keeping," Scholar said, slowly unscrewing the end piece from the tube.

"I can probably figure out where he got it," Lehash said, watching with the others.

Scholar gingerly tipped the canister, allowing the rolled scroll to fall out into his waiting hand. "It was given to the Founder when he established the first safe haven for our kind." Slowly he began to unroll the scroll, revealing the angelic script upon the golden parchment.

"It's a spell," Lorelei said, bending over to examine the writing.

"Yes, it is," Scholar said. "The first spell of concealment ever to be placed upon our sanctuary. The Malakim who visited approved of what Belphegor was doing and gave us his blessing, which meant God's blessing."

"Well, I'll be damned," Lehash said, pushing closer for a look. "A real live Malakim gave that to Belphegor." The gunslinger smirked. "Always wondered if we had God on our side; didn't know we had the paperwork to prove it."

Aaron came closer, moving past Lehash's bulk to stand next to Scholar. He gazed down upon the scroll, a strange look in his eyes. "A Malakim wrote this?" he asked, his index finger tracing the shape of the heavenly alphabet in the air above the scroll.

"Yes," Scholar answered.

"Then that means he touched it," the boy

said dreamily, his thoughts seemingly some-place else altogether.

"Of course he touched it," Scholar responded testily. "How else could he have written it?" He lifted his hand, allowing the scroll to roll shut.

"I have an idea," Aaron said, turning to leave. "It's probably a long shot, but it can't hurt to try."

"Where you going, kid?" Lehash asked, fol-lowing close behind.

"To see Gabriel."

chapter eight

"Time is short," Verchiel hissed, his voice echoing through the abandoned church. "Find the last of the Malakim."

Katspiel convulsed violently upon the unconsecrated altar of Saint Athanasius Church. His eyeless gaze stared blindly at the fading image of Heaven painted on the high rounded ceiling, his face wan, twisted in a mask of agony. The magicks the Archon attempted to command were wild and unruly, leaching away his life force in exchange for the location of the last of Heaven's magick users.

"So elusive," he grunted, reaching up with clawed hands as if to rend the air. "Quicksilver—moving from here, to there, across the world of God's man, then gone, like darkness chased away with the coming dawn."

The angel curled into a tight ball. "I must rest," he slurred.

But Verchiel would not hear of it. He flew from his perch on the back of a wooden pew and landed upon the altar beside the quivering Archon. "There will be no rest until the Malakim is found," he screeched, grasping Katspiel by the scruff, yanking him, flailing, into the air.

"Mercy," the angel mage begged, his voice trembling. "All I ask is for some time to—"

"Don't you understand, worm?" Verchiel growled, pulling the Archon closer to his snarling face. "Surprise is lost to us. Our prey knows he is being hunted."

"So tired . . . ," Katspiel groaned as he dangled limply in his master's grip.

"There will be plenty of time to rest once the Malakim is found and the final piece of knowledge is extracted from his skull." Verchiel dropped him to the dusty floor. "Continue," he ordered.

Slowly Katspiel raised his arms, a spell of summoning upon his lips, the drone of his feeble voice drawing down magickal forces eager to partake of his already depleted life force.

Verchiel watched intently until the sound of someone entering the church distracted him. He turned and saw Kraus heading down the center aisle toward him. The human moved differently now, his newly regenerated sensory organs taking in everything, devouring the sights around him.

Kraus approached the altar, and Verchiel watched curiously as a look of horror slowly spread across his face. "What is it, healer?" And then he, too, realized what the healer saw.

Verchiel had started to bleed.

New wounds had appeared, and old wounds, long since healed, had reopened, dark blood raining down to spatter upon the altar and puddle at the angel's feet.

"Time is short," he had told the Archon.

Truer words were never spoken.

The air around the sleeping girl crackled with a subdued supernatural energy, and Aaron could feel the hair on his arms and the back of his neck stand on end. Vilma was lying on a bare mattress on the floor, placed in the basement of an abandoned house on the outskirts of Aerie, away from the citizens' homes. She looked small upon the king-size mattress—fragile, as if the power inside her was consuming her mass, eating away at all that was human so only the angelic would remain.

A sheen of sweat was on her brow, and she grumbled in her sleep. But the language she spoke was neither English nor her native Portuguese. It was the language of angels, and Aaron knew that the essence inside her was growing stronger despite the supernatural restraints placed upon her.

Gabriel lay faithfully by Vilma's side, his dark brown eyes never leaving her as she slept. His burns had already begun to heal, the scorched patches filling in with new golden yellow fur.

"How is she?" Aaron asked, reaching out to stroke the dog's head.

"It's hurting her," he replied, his voice full of concern. *"I'm trying with all my might, but I can't seem to calm it down. It wants to get out—it wants to run wild."* The dog looked away from his charge to hold Aaron in his soulful gaze. *"But I'm not going to let that happen."*

"You're a good dog, Gabriel," Aaron said, and leaned down to kiss the top of his hard, bony head. "What would I do without you?"

The dog seemed to take the statement literally. *"What a horrible thought."* He tilted his head to one side considering the alternate reality. *"What* would *you do without me?"*

Aaron smiled, amused by the animal's strange perception of things. But the humor was fleeting as they again found themselves staring at the unconscious Vilma, locked within the grip of a power older than creation.

"What are they doing to help her?"

Aaron sighed. "That's just it, Gabe," he began. "They have no idea what to do. Normally, when something like this happens they . . ." He couldn't bring himself to say it.

"They what?" Gabriel asked. *"They wouldn't hurt Vilma, would they?"* He climbed to his feet. *"I won't let them, Aaron."*

"They don't want to, but it might come to that if something can't be done," Aaron explained. "She's becoming dangerous, Gabe, and to keep her from hurting someone . . . there might be no choice."

The Lab sniffed at the girl's sleeping body, his tail beginning to wag. *"She doesn't want to hurt anybody, and neither does the thing inside her. It just needs to be trained."*

"I know that. Look, Gabe, there is a slim possibility that certain angels called the Malakim might be able to help Vilma, but the thing is, nobody knows where they are."

Aaron could practically hear the gears clicking in Gabriel's square head as he tried to process the information.

"We have to find them, then," the dog said matter of factly.

"Exactly," Aaron replied. "Since your accident," he continued, "since I made you better, your senses have gotten more powerful, haven't they?"

"Yes."

"Do you think you could track an old scent from something?" Aaron asked.

The dog thought for a moment. *"How old?"*

Aaron shrugged. "I'm not sure. A few thousand years maybe."

"Is that all?" the dog responded, a mischievous twinkle in his dark brown eyes. *"And here I was thinking you were going to give me something tough."*

Something was drawing Lucifer out of his inner self, pulling him away from the retreat he had created deep within his subconscious. He didn't want to leave, struggling against the current threatening to wrench him from his internal world and the woman he loved, but it was to no avail. So he left Taylor standing nervously before the locked vault door and promised to return as soon as he was able.

He allowed himself to be drawn upward, the powerful force dragging him through multiple layers of consciousness, and the closer he got to the surface, the worse the pain became. But he endured, embracing it, for it had been his constant companion since his fall. It was his penance, and he deserved no less.

Lucifer's eyes opened, dried discharge crackling as his upper lid pulled away from the lower. He blinked away the blurriness, his burning gaze focusing upon the mystical circle that had been drawn on the parquet floor beneath him. An aching pain in his arms and legs diverted his attentions elsewhere, and he realized that he was suspended by chains, hanging over an arcane protective circle, the subject of some kind of ritual.

It was more than mere physical pain he felt; this unpleasant sensation went far deeper than that, and he came to the frightening realization that Verchiel was somehow succeeding with his mad plans—that the angel had found a way to undo God's Word. The image of the large vault door within his mind—its locks falling away— filled his head, and he recoiled from it.

"You can't do this," he said aloud, struggling pathetically against his bonds, his body swaying with his useless efforts.

"Oh, but I can," said a disturbing voice from close by, and Lucifer lifted his head to look upon Verchiel, or at least he believed it to be him.

Clad in armor that once shone like the sun, the figure that shambled toward him was a nightmare to behold. The exposed flesh of the angel's face, arms, and legs was wrapped in bandages, bloodied by oozing wounds.

"Is that you, Verchiel?" Lucifer asked, struggling to keep his head up, the muscles in his neck beginning to cramp. "What happened? Cut yourself shaving?" Then he saw the eyes that raged from between the gore-stained bandages and knew exactly who it was before him.

"Insolent even in the face of your own demise," Verchiel hissed.

In all his years of existence, Lucifer had never seen such hate as he now saw in the Powers leader. Here was a being birthed by God that had somehow lost touch with everything that made him a creature of the divine. Even Lucifer still remembered what it was like to serve God, after all that he had been through.

"Believe it or not, Morningstar, I asked the Archons to awaken you," Verchiel said, his voice a rasping whisper through the bandages that partially obscured his mouth. "I want you to be fully aware of the next catastrophic act you will be party to." The angel stepped closer, careful not to disturb the mystical circle, and grabbed Lucifer's chin, lifting his face to gaze upon Verchiel's disturbing visage. "I thought we might have a private discussion first, while the Archons rest. They have been working so very hard to complete their task."

"What's happened to you?" Lucifer asked. The sickening smell of decay wafted from Verchiel's body, and he wanted to turn his head away, but the Powers commander still held his chin firmly in hand.

"This is yet another example of how the Lord rewards those who serve Him faithfully," Verchiel growled bitterly. "All my wounds, received in service to His holy cause, open again and weeping."

Lucifer directed his gaze to Verchiel's cold eyes. "Do you think maybe He's trying to tell you something?" he asked, hoping to reach even a sliver of sanity in the Powers commander.

"Yes," Verchiel said with a slow nod of his bandaged head. "Yes, I do believe that He is attempting to commune with me. Through His actions, or lack there of, He is telling me that the sinful have won, that the wretched and the cursed, the criminals and the abominations whose taint has poisoned the heavens above and the earth below, hold indomitable sway over all."

Verchiel leaned his face closer to Lucifer's, the smell of rot nearly suffocating. "But I will not hear of it," he said, squeezing his prisoner's chin all the tighter, refusing to allow him to look away. "I will not surrender to those who should have died beneath my heel. I shall see it all turned to Hell before I give it away."

And with the last pronouncement of his rage, Verchiel released his grip and backed from the circle. "And to think, the one that began it all—who brought war to Paradise, and still had the audacity to believe that his sins could be forgiven—shall be the instrument of my defiance." Verchiel studied the first of the fallen, the hint of a grotesque smile beneath the soiled wrappings. "It brings me a certain satisfaction to know that the prophecy will never be brought to term, that the founder of our misery will never find forgiveness at the hands of his son."

Lucifer couldn't bear to hear any more of the angel's rantings. He wanted to return to the darkness of oblivion, to the comfort of a precious memory in the shape of a love long lost. But there was something that Verchiel said that he did not quite comprehend. He strained to lift his head and look upon the Powers commander to ask the question.

"Forgiveness at the hands of *his son?*"

Verchiel chuckled, a wet rumbling sound. "Don't tell me that you didn't know, or at least suspect, Morningstar," he teased.

"What are you saying?" Lucifer struggled to ask, the Archon spell used to return him to consciousness wearing thin.

"Why, the Nephilim of prophecy, the one called Aaron Corbet—he is your son."

chapter nine

"*This place is much bigger on the inside,*" Gabriel observed as he strolled deeper into the seemingly endless room, his nails clicking on the bare, hardwood floors.

"At that first stack, take a . . ." Aaron started to tell him, but the dog was already on his way to finding the others.

"*Don't tell me, Aaron,*" Gabriel said, his nose skimming the surface of the floor. It sounded like a Geiger counter searching for dangerous levels of radiation as he followed the scent. "*Let me find them on my own.*"

Gabriel hadn't wanted to leave Vilma, fearing that his absence would cause the essence to awaken again. But he had finally agreed when Aaron explained that it was the only way left to help the girl. Besides, Scholar wouldn't allow the scroll to leave his house.

Aaron followed the dog through the multiple winding corridors of bookshelves as the animal tracked his quarry. He was pleased with how well Gabriel was doing, but were the Lab's olfactory senses really good enough to find an angelic being that had left his scent on a scroll thousands of years ago? That was the million-dollar question, and a chance they were going to have to take.

Scholar had scoffed at the idea, saying that he'd never heard of anything quite so ridiculous, and the others weren't quite ready to go along for the ride either. Aaron defended his theory, giving examples of his dog's ability to track. Being able to find a slice of cheese hidden somewhere in a house didn't have quite the impact that he had imagined, but the example of Gabriel being able to track the scent of fallen angels was at least met with a begrudging curiosity. He explained that Gabriel's senses had intensified since he had been healed and that he was no longer just a dog. Gabriel was special and was capable of amazing things.

The dog suddenly stopped short, sniffed the air, and reversed his direction. *"Almost lost it,"* he grumbled. *"Lots of other smells around here, but I can smell that cigar stink above them all."*

And with that final statement, the dog quickened his pace, Aaron almost jogging to keep up. At a closed door he began to bark, his tail wagging furiously.

"Good dog," Aaron said, patting his head and opening the door to allow the animal to confront his prey.

They were waiting, sitting around a circular table. Lehash and Lorelei smiled as Scholar scowled.

"There's our mighty bloodhound," the gunslinger said, reaching out to give the dog a pet.

Gabriel licked his hand. *"I'm not a bloodhound. I'm a Labrador retriever, and I found you very easily because of your stink."*

The constable jokingly sniffed beneath his arms. "Didn't think I was that ripe, but maybe I was mistaken."

"I'm not impressed," Scholar said, adjusting the cuffs on his starched white shirt. "Sure, he was able to find us in here, but I'm curious to see his level of success when taking on the whole world."

Gabriel walked around the table until he was standing in front of Scholar. He sat down at the fallen angel's feet, never taking his eyes from him. *"We'll never know until we try, will we?"* the dog said, his voice filled with far more insight than Aaron would have imagined.

"He's right," Lorelei said, trying to hide her amusement. "We've gotta at least let him try. What can it hurt?"

The scroll had been returned to its protective canister and Scholar tentatively reached for it. "I feel just as strongly about the presence of animals in my place of work as I do about cigar smoke."

Lehash rolled his eyes, folding his arms across his chest. "Just let the dog sniff the damn scroll."

Scholar carefully slid the piece of parchment out of the tube and into his hand. Gabriel's head craned toward it, sniffing the air, and Scholar recoiled, pulling the scroll away.

"That's close enough," he snapped.

"No, it isn't," Gabriel told him.

Aaron stepped forward, holding his hand out to Scholar. "Give it to me," he said firmly.

Scholar started to object, but Lehash shifted in his chair, his steely gaze intense. "You heard the boy," he drawled menacingly.

As if it was the hardest thing he ever had to do, Scholar placed the rolled parchment in the center of Aaron's hand. The Nephilim knelt down beside the dog and began to unroll the scroll.

"That's much better," Gabriel said as Aaron placed it beneath his wet, pinkish nose. *"It smells very old."*

Aaron could feel Scholar's tension behind him as a bead of moisture began to form beneath one of Gabriel's nostrils, threatening to drip onto the priceless document.

"Easy there, Scholar," Lehash warned, "or you just might piss yerself."

"I'm done," the dog said, and Aaron moved

the scroll away just as the glob of moisture rolled from Gabriel's nose and dripped harmlessly to the floor.

"That wasn't so bad, was it?" Lorelei chided as Aaron handed the parchment back to Scholar.

The angel said nothing, quickly rolling the scroll up tightly and placing it back inside its protective container.

"Well?" Aaron asked for them all as he turned to Gabriel. The anticipation level in the room was extremely high. Much was riding on the dog, and Aaron wasn't quite sure how he would handle the situation should Gabriel fail. What would happen to Vilma then? He didn't want to think about that. Instead he focused on the Lab.

The dog ignored his question, getting up from where he sat and walking around the room in a circle, head bent back and sniffing the air.

"The anticipation is freaking killin' me, dog," Lehash growled, but Gabriel didn't pay him the least bit of attention as he continued to wander about the room.

Suddenly the dog let out an enormous sneeze, paused, and then sneezed again. "*I have it*," he said, his voice flat, and Aaron was about to get excited when he noticed that the hackles had risen on the back of his friend's neck.

"What is it, Gabriel?" he questioned, kneeling beside the dog. "What's wrong?"

"*I know where the Malakim is.*" The dog

looked nervously about the room, his ears flat against his head. *"And it is someplace very strange."*

Katspiel did not know how much longer he had.

The magick had given him the information he so desperately sought, but now it demanded payment, and he no longer had the strength to hold it at bay. The forbidden was in him, moving about freely, completely unhindered, partaking of flesh and blood, bone and spirit—all that defined him.

He was an Archon, an angel endowed with the facility to wield the mystical arts of Heaven. Not all were seen fit to wear this mantle, only a few selected by the mighty Malakim. Katspiel was one such being, and over time he learned the protean nature of the power he would attempt to tame.

It was killing him now, but he was left with little choice. It was either die as the conjuring nibbled away at his life force, or be brutaly killed by the displeased rage of Verchiel. Either way, Katspiel knew it was only a matter of time now before his life came to an end.

The Archon rose unsteadily to his feet upon the church altar, swaying in the darkness that had become his world since the magicks he sought to sunder, bound to the fallen angel Lucifer by the hand of God, lashed out and took away his eyes. He and his brethren should have stopped then, heeding the Creator's warning, stepping away from Verchiel's mad plan. But they had come to call the Powers leader "master," their existences inexorably intertwined, their fates becoming as one.

The location of the last Malakim burned in his mind, and Katspiel summoned his wings before it was too late. Enshrouding himself within their feathered embrace, he went to his master, all the while trying to imagine what the world would be like after the Word of God was undone and Lucifer's punishment was set loose upon the land. And as his wings opened in the school and he sensed that he was in the presence of Verchiel and the first of the fallen, Archon Katspiel realized that he was glad he would not be alive to experience it.

"Master Verchiel," he announced, hearing the sounds of an angelic being in the grip of torment, and the low, rumbling laugh of his master. "The last of the Malakim has been found," he managed, and slumped to the floor, the muscles beneath his decrepit flesh no longer capable of sustaining his weight.

"You have served me well, Katspiel," Verchiel said, an eerie calm in his voice, perfectly at ease with the horror his command would soon unleash. "And your loyalty shall be remembered long after the punishment is meted and order is restored to the heavens above and the earth below."

Oh yes, Katspiel was certain that the commander of the Powers was correct in that. He and his brothers would indeed be remembered for what they had done.

Remembered in infamy.

It nearly killed him to see her this way.

Aaron carefully sat down on the mattress beside Vilma. She had kicked away the light covers they had provided for her, writhing and moaning as if caught in the grip of a bad dream. Her breathing was shallow, and the golden manacles covering her wrists sparked and hummed as the power inside her tested the limits of angel magick. She had become more restless since Gabriel had gone, but his canine friend was needed elsewhere if they were going to help her.

The girl let out a pathetic cry and thrashed her head upon the pillow. A single tear broke loose from the corner of one tightly closed eye and trailed down the side of her face. He felt a hitch of emotion become trapped painfully in his chest and reached out to take hold of one of her hands. It felt warm and dry in his, and Aaron tried with all his might to infuse some of his own strength into her.

"Hey," he whispered, not wanting to startle or scare her. "Just wanted to stop by and see you before I leave. But I'll be back as soon as I can. I promise."

He wasn't sure if she was even able to hear

him, but it didn't matter. He needed to talk to her, needed to show himself why he was doing what he was about to do. If there was any doubt, he didn't recall it now.

"We're going to look for an angel—a Malakim, they're called—and I think he might be able to help you."

Vilma seemed a little calmer, and he liked to think that maybe it was because of his presence. Aaron knew it wasn't his fault, but he couldn't help feeling a certain amount of guilt. This wasn't what a beautiful, eighteen-year-old woman's life was supposed to be like. She should have been thinking about finals, graduation, and the prom, not about whether an angelic force from Heaven living inside her was going to cause her to go insane.

He rubbed his thumb gently across the back of her hand. "So I need you to hang on for me, to be strong, 'cause there's still a lot of things we need to talk about once you get better."

Vilma's life had been turned upside-down by her association with him. He felt like a kind of super virus, infecting anybody that got too close. *The casualty rate of the Aaron Corbet disease is pretty high,* he realized, thinking about all those who had died just for being part of his life: his foster parents, his psychologist, Stevie, Zeke, Camael, and Belphegor. Squeezing her hand tighter, Aaron decided that he wasn't going to let Vilma become part of that depressing statistic. He would rather die himself than have anything else bad happen to her.

Aaron released her hand, letting it gently fall to her side. He had to leave; the others would be waiting for him. He leaned forward, placing a tender kiss upon her forehead. "I'm so sorry for this," he whispered. "And I'm going to do everything that I can to make it up to you."

She offered no response and that was fine with him. Vilma seemed to be resting peacefully at the moment, and he took that as a sign for him to take his leave. Quietly he stood, his eyes never leaving her sleeping form, and backed away. He turned and just about jumped out of his skin when he saw that Lorelei was standing at the foot of stairs, her plastic makeup case, filled with angelic remedies, in hand. He hadn't heard her come down, and he put his hand against his chest to show that she nearly gave him a heart attack.

"Sorry," she whispered. "I didn't want to wake her."

Aaron looked back to the girl upon the mattress. "That's okay. She's sleeping pretty well now." He continued to stare at her, his heart aching.

"I don't want to state the obvious, Aaron," Lorelei said, "but you *do* know that this isn't your fault, right?"

He didn't answer, not fully believing that what she said was true.

"What's happening to Vilma would have occurred whether you were in the picture or not." She reached out and laid a supportive hand on his shoulder. "She's a Nephilim, Aaron, and you didn't make her that, no matter how guilty you feel."

He thought about all that Vilma had been through. "Verchiel used her to get at me. I should have—"

"Verchiel just made an already complicated situation a little more complicated," Lorelei interrupted. "No matter how rotten you think you are, Vilma's better off having you in her life than not. We all are."

He took his eyes from Vilma and looked at the Nephilim with the snow-white hair whom he had learned to trust as a friend and confidant. "Do you really think so?" he asked, the weight of his responsibilities feeling perhaps the tiniest bit more manageable.

She laughed softly and smiled at him. "I'm Lehash's daughter, for Pete's sake. I wouldn't say it if it weren't true."

He took it for what it was worth, and at that moment its value was quite high. "Thanks," Aaron said, turning back to Vilma for one final glance. "Take good care of her until I get back, would ya?" he asked Lorelei as he started up the stairs.

"You just worry about finding the Malakim and getting what we need," Lorelei responded. "Right now Vilma should be the least of your worries."

And she was right, Aaron knew as he walked down the hallway and out the front door. They were waiting for him on the front walk, Gabriel wagging his tail as the boy pulled the door closed behind him and stepped off the porch.

"Ready?" Aaron asked, a nervous sensation forming in the pit of his stomach.

"I was ready about fifteen minutes ago," Lehash grumbled, finishing up the last of a cigar. "Now I'm just plum chompin' at the bit."

"What's 'chompin' at the bit'?" Gabriel asked the angel.

"Ants in my pants," he responded, flicking the smoldering remains of his cigar to the street.

"You don't really have ants in your pants, do you?" the dog asked, confused by this new expression. *"If you do, you should get them out before they bite you."*

"Thanks for the advice," Lehash snarled, not having the patience to explain to the animal any further.

Aaron decided that it was time and called upon the power that was his birthright. Flexing the muscles in his back, he eased his wings from beneath the flesh and opened them to their full, impressive span.

"Group hug," he said, surprised at his own attempt at levity. "Let's do this."

The gunslinging angel and dog huddled closer. And he took them within his wings' ebony embrace, departing Aerie on a mission most dire, the fate of the woman he loved hanging in the balance.

chapter ten

"Hard day at the office?" Taylor asked.

Lucifer found himself back within his psyche. It was good to be away from the physical pain, even though he was beginning to feel an uncomfortable sensation in his chest. He wondered how long it would be before the pain found him, even this deep within the psychic landscape of his own fabrication.

They were sitting at a small kitchen table, very much like the one at which they had shared many a pleasant meal. And as in the past, this Taylor, this creation of Lucifer's fevered mind, had made a nice candlelit dinner.

The first of the fallen shuddered as the light of the twin candles illuminated a large door floating in the darkness around them. He studied the thick steel monstrosity created by his psyche to keep at bay the horrors of what he had done in Heaven. *Has it lost more of its padlocks and chains?* he worried.

He was sure it had.

"What, you're not going to answer my question?" Taylor asked as she picked up her napkin and placed it on her lap.

"I think Verchiel is succeeding," Lucifer said, eyeing the door. He could have sworn he heard movement on the other side. "He's found a way to undo the Word of God."

Taylor cut into her meal as she spoke: steak with mushrooms and thick, brown sauce. He loved mushrooms. "We can't allow him to do that." She primly placed a large piece of meat into her beautiful mouth, and he watched her chew as he considered his response. She was thin—dainty, really—but the girl could eat, and enjoyed doing so without the slightest hint of concern, he remembered fondly.

"No, we can't. But I don't know how long we'll be able to hold out." He knew the meal was only a fabrication of his thoughts, but it looked fabulous, and he dug in hungrily. "It's only a matter of time before he has everything he needs to set it free," he said, hearing another padlock fall.

Two glasses of red wine appeared on the table, and Lucifer watched Taylor pick hers up in a delicate hand and take a small sip. "Not that that isn't enough," she said, setting down her glass. "But is anything else bothering you?"

Something on the other side of the door pounded three times, and another lock clacked open to dangle uselessly from the end of a link of chain. "He told me that I sired a child. I have a son."

Taylor didn't respond; she simply cut another piece of meat. How could anything he said to her be a surprise? After all, she *was* a creation of his imagination.

"How did I not know this?" he asked, pushing his plate away, his appetite suddenly gone.

"Remember, there was time when you no longer wanted to be the Morningstar, when you attempted to abandon your true nature," Taylor responded as she picked up the napkin in her lap and dabbed at the corners of her mouth. She had cleaned her plate.

"It was when I was with you," Lucifer said. The door suddenly trembled, and he felt the vibrations of the assault as something hurled its weight against it.

Taylor smiled at him and nodded. "And you almost did forget," she said, crossing her long legs and letting the simple sandal she wore dangle from her foot. "We were happy—at least, I thought we were."

Lucifer felt a pain blossom in his chest and almost mistook it for God's Word coming undone, until he realized that it was the agony of his heart breaking yet again with the memory of leaving her. "I started to have dreams—about what I had done, the lives that were lost because of me—and I feared for your safety."

He stood and moved around the table toward her. She rose to meet him and they gently embraced. "It was never my intention to hurt you," Lucifer said, holding her tightly. "But I was insane to think that I could ever experience happiness after what I'd done," he whispered. "My penance wasn't finished, so I *had* to leave, for your sake as well as mine."

The door shook upon its hinges and more locks fell as Taylor looked up into his eyes. "You've seen him, haven't you? Our child."

Lucifer remembered the vision he'd had soon after being captured by Verchiel and becoming aware of the Nephilim prophecy. It was the image of a young man, a big yellow dog faithfully at his side. "Yes," he answered dreamily. "I think I have."

"His name is Aaron," Taylor said, laying her head against his chest. "It means exalted—on high."

Lucifer smiled and kissed her gently on the top of her head.

And the door vibrated threateningly as the punishment of God raged upon the other side.

Aaron had always believed that he shared a special, almost psychic bond with Gabriel, and that had only been intensified after the emerging power of the Nephilim saved the dog's life. The boy was testing this theory as they traveled through the void between an angel's place of departure and its final destination. The two had already shared dreams, so Aaron figured sharing thoughts in the waking world wasn't all that far-fetched.

As they left Aerie, he had asked the dog to think about what he had seen while sniffing the ancient scroll and to direct those thoughts to him. It was an overwhelming experience. Aaron's mind was bombarded with Gabriel's thoughts. At first they were simple, dealing with base needs like food, shelter, warmth, and companionship. But then they became more complex: recollections of places, events, important moments in the Labrador's life. Aaron had never imagined how much a game of fetch at the park had meant to the dog, or having his stomach rubbed, or that piece of steak in the doggy bag from a fancy restaurant.

And Aaron saw himself through the eyes of his dog, and through those loving eyes he could do no wrong. If only he could be half the person the animal believed him to be, then he would be truly worthy of such adoration.

He was finally able to focus enough within the labyrinthine twists of Gabriel's thoughts to find what he needed. Here was where the scent from the scroll had brought them. It was a place unlike any other on Earth. In fact it wasn't on Earth at all, and he could see why the dog had been so spooked. Aaron took the image and made it his own—and he felt a hint of dizziness, like the descent from a great height in an elevator, before his wings opened to reveal their location.

"Would you look at that," Lehash said in awe.

"Are we in Heaven?" Aaron asked. He gazed with wonder over the rolling plains of golden grass, at the richest of royal blue skies. The gentle winds filled with soft, traipsing melodies were the most beautiful sounds he had ever heard.

"No," Lehash said, tilting his head back and sniffing the air. "Maybe a little piece of it, but not Heaven in its entirety."

"*The person who wrote the scroll is over that hill,*" Gabriel said from beside Aaron, his snout pointed into the breeze.

"Where do you think we are, Lehash?" Aaron asked as they turned and followed the Lab up a small hill.

"Looks to me like somebody built a little hideaway smack dab between the here and the there." The fallen angel removed his Stetson, combed back his long white hair with his fingers, and returned the hat to his head. "I'm surprised the dog was able to find it."

"*I'm very special,*" Gabriel reminded him.

"That you are," Lehash agreed, chuckling.

"I didn't expect anything like that," Aaron

said suddenly. They had reached the top of the hill and he was pointing down toward a tiny cottage with dark brown shingles, tarpaper roof, and a rock foundation. Clouds of thick gray smoke billowed out of a stone chimney, and he had the impression that it was probably quite cozy on the inside.

"After all you've seen lately," Lehash said leading them down the hill, "you can still be surprised?"

They stopped in front of the heavy wooden door.

"*He's in there,*" Gabriel assured them, his keen nose twitching as he sniffed the air.

"Should I knock?" Aaron asked the fallen angel beside him.

Lehash shrugged. "Can't hurt to be polite, I guess," he answered, and Aaron rapped his knuckles on the door.

They waited, and when no response came, the gunslinger leaned forward and added his own two cents. Still nobody answered.

"We don't have the time for this," Aaron said impatiently. He reached out, grasped the knob, and pushed the door open. It was very dark inside. "Hello?" he asked, his voice echoing strangely, and he quickly realized why. The room they entered was enormous, and he was reminded of Scholar's library, although the size and opulence of this room put the fallen angel's residence to shame.

"Son of a bitch," Lehash said, looking at the curved, hundred-foot ceiling and then the marble floor beneath their feet. "But then, what did I expect from a Malakim?"

Gabriel sniffed around the entrance, his claws sounding like tap shoes on the smooth stone floor, while Aaron admired the great stone pillars that flanked them on either side.

"How tall are these Malakim?" he asked, taking note of the gigantic double doors at the end of the hallway before them. The knockers, enormous lion heads holding thick metal rings, were at least thirty feet from the floor.

"They're extensions of God, fer cryin' out loud," the gunslinger growled. "They can be as tall as they like."

And as if on cue, the double doors were flung wide with a thunderous clamor that caused the great hall to tremble, and a creature the likes of which Aaron had never seen or imagined came barreling down the hall toward them. It was at least fifty feet tall and wore armor that shimmered and bubbled as if forged from molten metal. Its head was that of a gigantic ram, and it had wings the color of a desert sunset. In its equally prodigious hands, it clutched a fearsome battle-ax that Aaron guessed was at least three times as big as him. They barely leaped away in time as the ax descended in a blurred arc to cleave the marble floor. Though it missed them, the aftershocks of the impact shook the floor beneath them as if they were in the grip of a major earthquake and they struggled to stay on their feet.

"I will not be caught as my brethren were," the great beast-man roared as he yanked his weapon from the broken marble and prepared to strike again. "The knowledge you wish to pilfer shall remain with me and me alone!"

"Stop!" Aaron begged moving toward the Malakim, hands outstretched. "We just want to—"

But Lehash had summoned his pistols of angelic fire, and as the beast turned to deal with this new threat, one of its mighty wings lashed out and swatted Aaron away. He saw a galaxy of stars as he landed upon the stone floor, fighting to stay conscious. Seeing his master down, Gabriel leaped at the fearsome giant, sinking his fangs into the molten metal of the creature's armor, only to let go with a cry of pain as his mouth began to smoke and smolder.

Lehash's guns roared to life and bullets of heavenly fire exploded upon the berserker's armor, miniature explosions across the surface of the sun, but to little effect. The monster spread its wings wide and soared at Lehash. The fallen angel continued to fire his weapons as the armored beast swung his ax, the flat of the blade catching the gunslinger and sending him rocketing through the air into one of the great pillars. The constable lay still upon the cold, stone floor among pieces of the broken pillar as the beast touched down in a crouch beside him. Tossing the mighty ax from one hand to the other, it lifted the weapon above its head with a bellow of rage and prepared to finish its fallen foe.

Aaron struggled to his feet, feeling the transformation of his body to a more fitting form for battle. He didn't want it to be this way. All he wanted was to ask for help, but they were beyond that now, and combat was the only answer. He propelled himself forward, landing between Lehash and the ax. He listened to the great blade whistle as it cut through the air, his own sword of heavenly flame igniting in his hand to meet it. The sigils burned upon his flesh and he felt his wings explode from his back as the two awesome blades connected with a clamorous peal, the explosive force of the two weapons meeting tossing them apart. Aaron's ears rang. Quickly he struggled to his feet, ready to meet the next assault from the armored monster.

But the beast simply stood, the great battle-ax lowered to its side. It was staring at him, its cold animal gaze intensely scrutinizing. "It's you," it said, a strange smile briefly appearing upon its savage features.

"We don't mean you any harm," Aaron said carefully, and watched as the mass of the giant before him began to change, to diminish, the battle-ax fading away in a mellifluous flash of brilliance. No longer was there a fearsome warrior before him; it had been replaced by a tall, striking figure with silvery white hair and skin the color of copper.

"I am well aware of that . . . now," said the angelic being. "I am Raphael of the Malakim, and I beg your forgiveness." His voice was like the wind outside: melodic, strangely soothing. "I thought you to be servants of the renegade Verchiel, but of course you are not. There is no mistaking the sigils upon your body, son of the Morningstar."

Aaron allowed his weapon to dissipate. "You know about the whole Lucifer thing too, huh?" he asked as he walked over to check Gabriel. The dog's mouth was slightly blistered, but he appeared to be fine.

"The Malakim have known of your coming for a very long time," the angelic creature said simply, turning to walk back through the towering doorway. "In fact, we were responsible—my brothers and I—for providing the seer with the vision that described the prophecy of which you are such an important part."

Aaron watched the figure disappear into the room beyond as he hurried to Lehash's side. The fallen angel was sitting up amidst the rubble of the damaged pillar, rubbing the back of his neck and wincing in discomfort.

"Did you hear him?" Aaron asked excitedly as he helped the gunslinger to his feet.

"Always was curious as to who got the ball

rollin'," Lehash said, beating the dust from his clothing with his hat. "Makes sense it was them."

Raphael again appeared in the doorway. "Do hurry," he said, motioning with a delicate hand for them to join him. "We haven't much time, and there is still much to discuss." He disappeared again into the room beyond the enormous doors.

The three cautiously entered the room beyond the great hallway. Aaron couldn't believe his eyes—another bizarre example of angelic magick. From the regal majesty of the hall, to this: It was as if they had wandered into an old-fashioned parlor. The Malakim was sitting in the far corner at a small wooden desk, rummaging through one of the drawers. "Please, make yourselves at home," he said, busily searching for something.

"Impressive place you got here," Lehash said, looking about the room. The decor was warm and rich: lots of dark wood, and long velvet curtains that covered two sets of windows, the thick, red material draping down to the polished hardwood floor.

Gabriel hopped up on a sofa, upholstered in the crimson material and framed in shiny, dark wood.

"Gabriel, get down!" Aaron ordered automatically.

"But he said to get comfortable," the dog

protested as he slowly slunk from his place upon the furniture.

"That's quite all right," the Malakim said, shutting the drawer and rising to approach them. "That's what our little hideaway has always been about," he said, lifting his robed arms and gesturing about the room. "A place for my brethren and I to get away from our duties, to relax and ponder what we have seen."

Gabriel lay down upon an embroidered area rug and with a heavy sigh placed his snout between his paws and closed his eyes. No matter where they were or what they were doing, that animal could always find the time to steal a little nap.

"Please, sit, relax. Use this place as it is supposed to be used."

Lehash politely removed his hat, and he and Aaron sat down upon the sofa vacated by Gabriel. The Malakim chose a leather chair across from them.

Aaron leaned forward tentatively. "You said something about your brothers and Verchiel?"

The Malakim nodded and lay his head against the back of the chair. "He killed them both, taking from them knowledge that is not meant for an angel of his caste."

Lehash appeared stunned. "Verchiel killed two a' you?" he asked incredulously. "He actually killed two Malakim? How is that even possible?"

The bronze skinned creature closed his eyes, his face twisting in pain as he recounted the tale.

"They took us by surprise, using powerful magicks that we ourselves taught the mages in his service."

For a moment the room was uncomfortably silent; Gabriel's heavy breathing was the only sound.

Raphael continued, smiling sadly as he opened his eyes. "With our ability to glimpse the future, you would think we should have been able to prepare for this. But then, maybe because it was inevitable, subconsciously we chose not to see it."

Aaron squirmed in his seat, images of Vilma in the throws of painful transformation filling his head. He was torn by the reason he had come on this mission and by what Verchiel was up to. Although his loyalty was to Vilma, he found it extremely disconcerting to learn that both he and the Powers commander seemed to be searching for the same thing.

"What does he want?" Aaron asked curiously. "What is he trying to take from you?"

The Malakim shifted in his chair and crossed his long legs. "At first I had no idea, but now it makes perfect sense." He reached inside the folds of his robe and brought forth a vial of glass, its ends sealed with ornate golden metal. Aaron could see that there was liquid inside as the Malakim passed it to him. "Before our time is up, however, this is for your mate," he said as Aaron took the offering.

Aaron blinked repeatedly, unsure if he had heard the angel correctly. "Mate?" he asked.

Raphael nodded as he sat back in his seat. "Yes, your mate. And may I be the first to say that your children will be absolutely magnificent."

Fifty thousand volts of electricity could have passed through Aaron's chair and it would have had pretty much the same effect upon him.

"My children?" he yelped, shocked by the Malakim's words.

Gabriel sat up suddenly, awakened by his master's exclamation. *"What's happening?"* the dog questioned in a grumbling bark, looking about the room. *"What's going on?"*

"I think your master just got a little peek at the future," Lehash said, amusement in his gruff voice. He reached down and patted the dog's head. "That's all."

"No," Gabriel said emphatically. *"Can't you hear it?"* he asked, his nose twitching, hackles of fur rising around his neck. The dog rose, his body trembling in anticipation.

The Malakim sighed, standing from his chair. "It all seems so brief," he said sadly, brushing the wrinkles from the front of his robe, "when finally confronted with your inevitable demise."

Aaron was about to ask for an explanation when he heard it as well. He knew the sound; it was the noise made when an angel traveled from one place to another, implosions of sound as the fabric of reality was torn open for a brief instant and allowed to flow shut. Only this time he heard it multiple times, and understood exactly what it meant.

"We're under attack," he blurted out as winged shapes exploded into the room from beneath the velvet curtains in a shower of glass and fire.

"No kidding," Lehash growled. His pistols flashed to life in his grasp and he began to fire.

The sigils had risen upon Aaron's flesh and an idea for a weapon had entered his thoughts, when he felt a powerful grip upon his arm. He turned to confront Raphael, who was shaking his head.

"You are to leave here now," he said above the roar of Lehash's guns and Gabriel's frantic barks.

Aaron started to protest, but the look upon the angelic sorcerer's face rendered him speechless. "There is nothing you can do for me now. Return to Aerie, help your mate, and meet your own destiny," the Malakim ordered.

Aaron chanced another look at his friends. The Powers soldiers had momentarily stopped their charge through the windows, but Gabriel and Lehash stood at the ready, just in case. *The calm before the storm.*

"Take your friends and go," Raphael told him.

And though it pained Aaron to leave the heavenly being, he knew that things far larger than him were at work here. "C'mon. We have to go," he called to his friends as the black wings that would take them back to Aerie emerged from his back.

The Malakim bowed his head to Lehash and Gabriel as they passed him, his body already changing, his gentle features becoming more animal, the molten armor again appearing on his expanding form.

Aaron was about to take his companions into his winged embrace when the wall of the room exploded inward and more Powers soldiers surged in. Raphael met the attack with unbridled fury, Powers soldiers dying beneath the bite of his monstrous ax.

And then Aaron saw him, the focal point of the young Nephilim's rage, portions of his body not covered in armor wrapped in bandages stained with gore. Verchiel entered the room behind his troops, spear of fire clutched in his hands, tattered wings beating the air as he searched for his chosen prey. Aaron knew he should have left then, but he hesitated, held in place by his hatred for the leader of the Powers host.

The Malakim turned, as if sensing that they had not yet gone. "Go," he bellowed in a voice like the roar of a jungle cat. "It is not time for the final conflict. Go!"

And as Aaron closed his wings, he witnessed the most horrible of sights: The Powers swarmed upon Raphael, cutting down the Malakim in a senseless flurry of savagery. Verchiel strode passed the violence, fixated upon the Nephilim.

"Leave!" Aaron heard the last of the magickal trinity cry out from beneath the angelic swarm. He finally did as he was told, taking his companions within his wings' embrace.

"Not this time," Verchiel screeched, letting fly the javelin of fire with all his blistering rage and fury behind it.

Aaron wished them back to Aerie.

But the angel's spear was faster.

chapter eleven

Kraus awoke curled beneath a tattered blanket on the floor, a scream of terror upon his lips.

For a moment he thought the darkness had claimed him again, that perhaps Verchiel had taken back his wonderful gift, but then realized that it was only the night collected around him. Empty bookcases and stacked metal desks emerged from the gloom as his new sight adjusted to the inky black of nighttime.

He had been dreaming, vividly recalling a time before his service to his lord and master, Verchiel. A time of woe and suffering.

Tossing back his blanket, he climbed to his feet and stood in the darkness of the room. Something was wrong; he could sense it. There was an unnatural hum, a pulsing throb like the beat of some prehistoric monster's heart in the air around him. The sound was everywhere—it *needed* to be everywhere—and he felt the desperation of it worming inside him, bringing forth further memories of the dark times before he swore his fidelity to God's warrior and his holy mission.

Kraus left the room, seeking to escape the recollections of his early days of torment, to distract himself elsewhere, but the alien thrum was with him, no matter where he went, rousing memories of a past long suppressed.

Before serving the Powers, all he had known was darkness and pain, the pity and the disdain of the sighted. He had been raised in a place very much like this one, very much like the Saint Athanasius Church and Orphanage had been before its doors were closed.

The Perry School for the Blind. It was the only home he had ever known.

Kraus moved down the darkened corridors, riding the intensifying waves of unease. He could not keep the past at bay; the memories escaped, bursting up from layers of time, as vivid as if they had occurred only moments before.

There had been others like him at the Perry School, born without sight, given up to those who cared for the less fortunate. And care they did. Oh yes, he remembered their care indeed.

Kraus approached an open door and a staircase that led down into deeper darkness. The feeling was stronger here, and he descended, drawn toward the wellspring of despair, all the while remembering.

The staff at the school for the blind treated them as lesser life forms, below even the ferocious dog kept by Mr. Albert Dentworth, the head administrator. Kraus relived the terror that would grip him every time he heard the rattling of the animal's chained collar and its nails clicking and clacking on the hardwood floors as it drew closer. They were nothing but burdens to the world and to the personnel whose job it was to care for them, and were often told as much. For the majority of his existence he lived in Hell, and every night he prayed to be brought to Heaven.

The stairway took him to the gymnasium and into the lair of the Archons. At the moment, they were gone, off with Verchiel on his latest incursion. An intricate, mystical circle had been drawn upon the floor with what looked like dirt, and above it, from thick chains, the prisoner hung. A deep, vertical gash had been cut from the prisoner's chest to his stomach, the wound held open with metal clamps, and Kraus wondered how it was even possible that the prisoner still lived.

As a child, his every waking moment, and before going to sleep at night—exhausted from chores that left his fingers stiff and bleeding—Kraus had prayed for God to take him away. He didn't think himself more deserving than any of the others who lived beneath the roof of the Perry School, it was just that he'd had his fill and wanted it to stop. He couldn't live like that any longer, and each night he begged the merciful Creator to end his life.

The first of the fallen moaned pitifully, and a strange, red-colored cloud puffed from his open chest to be trapped within the confines of the mystical circle beneath. Kraus found himself driven back by an overwhelming sense of desolation that suddenly permeated the atmosphere. He had found the source of his waking malaise, and whatever it was, it came from within the body of the fallen angel Lucifer.

Kraus heard the angel that he would later call his master, as he had those many years ago—Verchiel, whispering in his ear, telling him he had been sent by God, and that because of his fervent prayers, he had been chosen to aid the soldiers of the Lord in the most important of missions.

Kraus remembered the incredible joy, the sheer euphoria of knowing that God had heard his pleas, but at the time he had been filled with great sorrow. He knew that only he would know this happiness, and those brothers and sisters in darkness with whom he had shared the hell of the Perry School would continue to know only suffering. How could he do the work of God, knowing that others like himself still suffered?

And the angel Verchiel had offered him a

solution. *"You can end their suffering,"* he had said. *"All you need do is command me, for this will be my payment to you, for the fealty you will swear to me. All you need do is ask."*

So Kraus had begged the messenger of Heaven to release the others of the Perry School from their lives of suffering and sorrow.

And Verchiel had obliged.

The memory of that night drove Kraus to his knees. He was trembling, awash in the raw, unconstrained emotions of that moment long ago. Whatever was leaking from the body of Lucifer, it was quite proficient in dredging up the echoes of the past.

Kraus recalled the night he was reborn as a servant of the Powers, pulled from the relative warmth of the school into the heights of the cold night sky, the sound of Verchiel's beating wings almost deafening. And he heard the cries of other heavenly creatures around him as he was carried higher and higher.

"They shall know suffering no longer," the angel who would be his master had roared, and the sky around them rumbled as if in agreement. The flash of lightning that followed somehow permeated the darkness that was his existence. He remembered the searing white light and the roar of thunder that shook the air.

Kraus gulped for air, his body sliding down the cool concrete of the gymnasium wall. The memories were unmerciful, his senses raw.

Somehow he could feel the lightning strikes upon the school, the smell of it as it burned filling his nostrils, the cries of those trapped within filling his ears.

He had always told himself that it was for the best. The students of the Perry School had been freed from a pathetic existence; he truly believed that. But lately he had begun to see things more clearly, and was filled with horror. Since Verchiel's gift to him, his perceptions were slowly changing, revealing the ugly reality of it all.

The air around him shimmered and quaked, and Kraus knew that his master had returned, but he did not feel joy as he would have in the past, only apprehension.

The angels appeared before him. There were fewer Powers soldiers, and those who remained mere shadows of their once glorious selves. They appeared haunted, the armor they wore hanging loosely upon their diminished frames.

And then there was Verchiel, the sight of him filling the healer with a strange mixture of sadness and fear. His once golden chest plate was tarnished almost black with the blood of his prey, and the freshly opened wounds continued to weep, saturating the bandages the healer had used to dress them.

Verchiel fell to his knees before the mystic circle. "The time is nigh," he said, and the remaining Archons scurried about their preparations.

But for what? Kraus wondered, an over-whelming feeling of dread reaching down to the depths of his soul. He wanted to ask the angel that was his lord and master, but he feared what the answer would be.

Aaron thought it had missed him.

He had hesitated for only a moment as he struggled with the idea that he could finally put this madness to rest once and for all. But the look upon the Malakim's face—the intensity in his dark, soulful gaze—had told him that he should leave, that perhaps a being that had lived for millions of years might have a better idea of the big picture than he did.

He honestly believed that Verchiel's spear of fire had passed harmlessly through the air where he and his friends had been standing moments before, confident his new abilities were far superior to the fiery weapon of the Powers commander. Aaron remembered closing his wings, hugging Lehash and Gabriel tightly against him and thinking of Aerie—seeing it as clear as day in his head. They had gotten away, free and clear.

Or so he thought.

With deadly accuracy, the spear made from the fires of Heaven had found its target.

He had made it back to Aerie, unfurling his wings and releasing his friends, before falling to his knees. Aaron couldn't seem to catch his breath, his body strangely numb, but he could hear everything they were saying. Lorelei was there, demanding to know what had happened as she knelt over him in the street. Lehash was close by, explaining the attack upon the Malakim's lair.

Aaron guessed that Lorelei was using some kind of magick on him, for he could feel her hands upon his chest probing at where *he imagined* the spear had nailed him. It really didn't hurt too badly; in fact he didn't feel much pain at all. *Maybe I'm just tired from all the running around,* he thought.

Gabriel was with him, nervously panting in his ear. Aaron wanted to tell his friend that everything was going to be all right, that he was fine, but for some reason he couldn't talk.

Everyone around him seemed to be in a panic.

Maybe I should be worried, he thought, but then dismissed it as foolish. He was fine; they would have him fixed up in no time.

They were carrying him now, bringing him to Lorelei's house. That was good, he thought as a heavy fatigue closed in around him. All he needed was some rest, and then he would be fine.

All he needed was rest.

"*He looks dead,*" Gabriel said flatly, sitting beside his master's bed. He had been by Aaron's side since they'd returned from their mission, scrutinizing every twitch, every movement—of which there was very little. This worried the dog, for Aaron was a very restless sleeper, and to see him lying so still was greatly disturbing.

"But he's not," Lorelei said, reaching down to scratch behind the dog's ear.

Gabriel moved his head away, too distracted for the affection of others. *"I know he's not dead,"* he replied, his eyes never leaving Aaron. *"Believe me, I'd know. I'm a dog; I'd smell it. Death has a very strong smell."*

They both fell silent. Lorelei leaned over to check Aaron's bandage as Gabriel watched closely. There had been very little blood, the intense heat of the spearhead cauterizing the wound almost instantly. She had put something on the injury, something that smelled very strange, very bitter. She had told him that it was an old medicine made from a root of the Tree of Knowledge, from a place called Eden. Gabriel didn't care for its scent—it made him sneeze and his eyes water—but if it was going to help Aaron, it was fine with him.

Vilma, on the other hand, was doing much better. The contents of the vial that Raphael had given Aaron seemed to be exactly what the girl had needed. The angelic essence had calmed almost immediately, and it appeared that she was going to be all right.

Gabriel was suddenly frustrated. He loved

Vilma very much and certainly did not want anything bad to happen to her. But if she got well and Aaron didn't, how would he feel toward her then? The dog pushed the thoughts aside, returning his attentions to his master.

"When will we know if he'll live?" Gabriel asked Lorelei as she continued to examine Aaron's wound.

The Nephilim gently replaced the bandage and moved away. "He's comfortable," she said with a slight shrug of her shoulders. "I'm keeping the wound clean to prevent any infection."

"But when will we know?" the dog barked, his demeanor far angrier than he had intended. He lowered his head, ashamed, his ears going flat against his blocky skull. *"I'm sorry I barked,"* he apologized. *"I'm just worried."*

"It's all right," Lorelei said with understanding, reaching to stroke his head again. This time he didn't pull away. "We've done all we can do."

"So we have to wait?" Gabriel turned to her as she continued to pet the short, velvety fur atop his head.

Lorelei nodded. "Afraid so."

He went back to watching Aaron, the very faint rise and fall of his chest, wishing with all his might for him to be well again.

"I'm going to go grab something to eat," Lorelei said. "Would you like to come with me?"

"No, thank you. I think I'll just stay here with him." Gabriel slowly lowered his face to rest his

chin upon the bed near Aaron's frighteningly still hand. *"I'm not feeling very hungry."*

The door that held back the outcome of the Morningstar's hellish folly shook violently on its psychic hinges.

It wanted out.

The great vault door moaned as it slowly began to bulge outward. All that remained was the steel itself: the locks, bolts, and chains, all broken by the fury of the maelstrom railing behind it.

Lucifer was alone now. Taylor was gone. She had left him when the pain in his chest had become too great, as if she couldn't bear to see what was going to happen.

No, he thought, on his knees before the psychic blockade. *I can't let it out.*

He concentrated upon the battered door and saw that there were new locks, sliding bolts, and thick black chains, all strong—or stronger than what had been there before.

Hell will not be released this day, the first of the fallen angels told himself, finding the strength to climb to his feet before the obstacle that separated the world from holocaust. All the pain, misery, and sorrow that he was responsible for would stay within him, where it belonged, where it had been placed. He'd always found it strangely amusing that the punishment given unto him by God had somehow managed to

become a thing of legend in the human world—
an actual place of eternal damnation for those
who sinned against their chosen religious faith.
Gehenna, Sheol, Ti Yu, Jahannam, Hades, Hell—
so many names for what was his and his alone to
bear.

The force upon the other side intensified,
and he was hurled backward by the savagery of
its furor. His new, stronger restraints were
ripped away, tossed into the darkness, ineffec-
tive against the relentless onslaught delivered
against the psychic representation of God's
Word.

The Morningstar crawled to his feet, trying
again to reinforce the barrier, but the sharp, biting agony in his chest drove him to his knees. He
looked down and saw the wound. A bloody,
twelve-inch gash had appeared there, and the
sight of it filled him with trepidation. He was
growing weaker, his strength draining from the
vertical opening carved in his center.

The door shuddered and vibrated within its
frame, and Lucifer watched in mute horror as
the top right corner started to bend outward, the
steel moaning and squealing its objection.

"Please, God, no," Lucifer hissed, throwing
himself at the door, pressing his body against it.
The pain, guilt, and sorrow of what his jealousy
caused had grown stronger through the millennia, and he had always found the strength to
keep it at bay within himself, for this was his

designated burden. Now he tried with all his might to will that barrier stronger, to add his mental strength to God's original penance, but could feel the awful vibrations of an unstoppable force through the many inches of what should have been super-strong metal.

From the twisted corner he first saw it, a tendril of luminescent vapor. Lucifer knew this thing intimately. It had been a part of him for what seemed like forever, fused to his angelic essence since his fall from grace. He knew its rage, its sorrow, and its infinite cruelty, and despaired for the fate of God's world if it were allowed to be free.

"Don't let this happen," he prayed, his faced pressed against the trembling metal, and he was glad that Taylor, even though a creation of his mind, was no longer there to witness his horrendous failure. "Please," he begged as the door buckled and the metal twisted. And he had just about given up all hope of stopping the deluge of Hell from flooding the world.

When there came a voice.

"Looks like you could use a hand here," it said, and Lucifer turned to gaze into the face of salvation.

It was a nice face—with *his* eyes.

chapter twelve

Verchiel listened intently to the powerful arcane words stolen from the minds of the Malakim as they spilled from the lips of the Archon faithful. *It is only a matter of time*, the Powers commander thought, amused that he was actually even aware of time's passage. He had existed since the dawn of creation and had never really given the concept much thought, until now.

The three remaining Archon magicians stood within the mystical circle beneath the suspended form of Verchiel's prisoner, his instrument of retribution. Everything was proceeding smoothly, the pieces of his mechanism for vengeance falling ideally into place, almost as if it were meant to be. *As if He knows that He must be punished for what He has allowed to transpire.*

The Archons droned on, the pilfered knowledge of the Malakim helping to unravel the edict

of God. Lucifer moaned in the grip of unconsciousness as the magickal obstructions holding
back his punishment were methodically peeled
away. The first of the fallen angels was fighting
them, but Verchiel would have expected no less
from one that had been the Creator's most
beloved—and greatest disappointment.

The Powers leader stepped closer to the
arcane ritual, careful not to open his own
wounds that had finally stopped bleeding.
"Give in, Morningstar," he urged the fallen
angel. "Accept your responsibility, not only for
the fall of Heaven, but now for the ruin of
mankind as well."

He strolled around the mystical circle,
around his despised adversary, the one whose
corruption had acted as a cancer, eating away at
Verchiel's holy mission—at everything that
defined his purpose in The Most Holy's blessed
scheme of things. "The pain you must have
experienced these countless millennia, my
brother," Verchiel cooed. "Now you have a
chance to be free of it—to let your punishment
be shared by all who have sinned."

Lucifer thrashed in his chains, droplets of
perspiration raining from his abused body to be
absorbed by the soil of Heaven that comprised
the magickal circle below him. His mouth trembled as he strained to speak.

"What is it, brother?" Verchiel asked in a soft
whisper. He leaned closer, eager to hear his pris-

oner voice his agony, perhaps even a plea for mercy. "Speak to me. Share with me your woes."

The fallen angel spoke. It was but two words, and spoken so softly that the leader of the Powers was not quite sure that he had heard it correctly.

"What was that again, Lucifer Morningstar?" Verchiel asked, leaning even closer to the first of the fallen's cracked and trembling lips.

"Thank you."

Verchiel recoiled as if struck. *Is this some kind of perverse game the criminal is playing?* he wondered. *Some bizarre way to show his strength? His superiority? It is all for naught if that be the case.*

"You thank me for this, monster?" he raged, feeling his own wounds begin to weep again. "For the torment you now endure?" His voice trembled with fury.

Lucifer was struggling to remain conscious, his eyes slowly rolling back in his head as the lids gradually began to fall.

"Tell me!" Verchiel shrieked, reaching in to the confines of the magickal circle to grab the fallen angel by his short, curly hair and yank his head toward him.

Lucifer's eyes snapped wide and a demented grin bloomed upon his tormented features.

"Tell me," Verchiel hissed again.

"If not for this . . . for you," the Morningstar whispered, "I would never have met my son."

† † †

The mouse's stomach ached from hunger. It had not foraged for food since its friend had been brought here to this room. It couldn't, not while the man was being tormented so.

In the shadows the mouse cowered, afraid to move. There was something in the air here, something unnatural that made its tiny heart flutter like a moth attempting to escape the spider's web. Every one of its primitive instincts screamed for it to run, that here was certain death. But it remained—afraid to abandon the one who had befriended it. Loyal to a fault.

They were hurting its friend again. The mouse did not want to watch, but could not tear its eyes away. It yearned to do something, anything to help the one who had shown it such friendship, but its tiny mind could not even begin to fathom what that something might be. It did not have the size or ferocity to frighten the larger, more powerful creatures, or the strength in its jaws to gnaw upon the thick metal chains. So it cowered in the shadows, watching and afraid.

Too small to matter.

Aaron wasn't sure what he expected of the fallen angel that was his father. He was *Lucifer*, after all, and all kinds of crazy stuff had passed through his mind: red skin, pencil-thin mustache, goatee, cloven hooves, horns, pointed tail, pitchfork. He was curious but never expected the answers to be imminent.

He knew that he was unconscious, in some dark, inner place, alone, or so he had believed. He had wandered through the shadows for quite sometime, descending deeper and deeper into the inner world of darkness, until he heard the cries for help.

"Please, God, no."

Instinctively Aaron moved toward the sound of the plaintive voice, cutting through the ocean of black.

"Don't allow this to happen."

In the distance he saw a man standing before an enormous metal door, pressing himself against its surface, as if trying to keep it from opening.

"Please," the stranger begged as something pounded and railed upon the other side.

Aaron felt compelled to help the man and tentatively approached. But as the man turned to face him, a smile that could only be described as euphoric spread across his handsome yet strained features. And in that moment Aaron knew this stranger's identity.

This was Lucifer Morningstar, the first of the fallen.

His father.

"I'm not sure how long he can hold out," Aaron muttered, opening his eyes and gazing up at the cracked and stained ceiling of the bedroom where he had been staying since coming to Aerie.

"You're awake," Gabriel said over and over again, licking his face, head, ears, and hands with abandon. *"You're awake. You're awake. You're awake."*

He wasn't sure how long he'd been unconscious. Gabriel's affection could not be used as an accurate guage. There were days Aaron had gone out to get something from his car and been met with the same kind of exuberant greetings, as if he had not seen the Lab in months.

Aaron pulled the dog's face away from his, scratching him behind the ears. "Hey, fella," he said. "Nice to see you, too. How long was I out?"

"About two days," answered a voice as the bedroom door opened and Lorelei walked in carrying a tray loaded with medical supplies. She placed the tray atop the dresser and retrieved a bottle of antiseptic, bandages, some cotton balls, and a roll of tape.

"I thought it was at least a week," Gabriel said as he lay down beside his master, rump pressed tightly against Aaron's side.

"It really is true what they say about animals having no concept of time," Lorelei said, sitting on the bed and carefully peeling the bandage from his bare chest.

"He has a tendency to exaggerate," Aaron said. "Will I live?"

"It was touch and go there for a while," she said honestly, examining the wound. "But it seems that you've healed up pretty well." She dabbed at the still-tender puncture in his chest with a cotton ball soaked in antiseptic. "Lehash told us what you did, hanging around a bit too long after the shit hit the fan. Very stupid, Aaron Corbet. If you're not careful, they'll revoke your savior's license." She placed a new bandage over the wound and taped it down.

"How's Vilma?" he asked, throwing off the thin sheet that covered him, starting to rise from the bed.

"Hey," the female Nephilim protested. "She's resting comfortably, which is exactly what you should be doing." She halfheartedly tried to push him back, but had little success.

Aaron felt a bit weak and dizzy, and placed his hand against the wall to steady himself. "There's no time for that," he said, waiting for the room to settle. "I'm not sure how much longer he can hold out." He moved to his duffel bag to dig out a new shirt.

"You said that before." Gabriel was still lying on the bed. *"Who are you talking about?"*

Aaron slipped a red T-shirt over his head and gently pulled it down over his chest, so as not to disturb the bandage. "While I was out, I went someplace," he said, putting on his socks and sneakers. "Inside here," his hands fluttered around the sides of his head before beginning to tie his sneakers. "And I met my father—I met Lucifer."

"You met the Morningstar?" Lorelei asked in shock.

Gabriel bounded from the bed to join Aaron by the door. *"Was he nice?"* he asked, tail wagging.

"I met him, and now I know what Verchiel is up to," Aaron said, leaving the bedroom. "And it's pretty horrible."

"Are you up for this, Aaron?" Lorelei asked as she followed him to the front door. "You almost died, and here you are running off again."

He stopped and stared at her, not really sure what to say.

"There's an awful lot riding on you and—"

"And none of it will matter if Verchiel has his way," Aaron interrupted.

Lorelei looked as though she might protest, but clearly thought better of it. "Promise me you'll be careful," she said instead.

"I'll be careful."

The woman nodded. "Good. You're the first savior I've ever had for a friend, and I'd hate to have to find another."

chapter thirteen

$\mathcal{I}$t had been a good visit.

Lucifer only wished that they could have done something a bit more pleasant, a few drinks perhaps, a nice dinner, conversation that went well into the wee hours of the morning. Holding back Hell was not the activity he would have chosen for his first meeting with his son.

He seems like a good kid, Lucifer mused. Eager to help, and he had his father's eyes, but there really wasn't much he could do about the Morningstar's current situation. He had only helped to delay the inevitable for a little while longer.

Things were bad. Vechiel's magicians had almost succeed in breaking down all his remaining barriers, and the pain was becoming unbearable. Lucifer hadn't wanted his son to see him this way, so he had sent him away, urging him to put his strength to use elsewhere, for his was a lost cause.

But deep down, the first fallen angel didn't want to believe that was completely true. The prophecy of forgiveness had come to fruition because of him, because he had hoped that someday the Lord God would understand how sorry he was and give him the chance to apologize.

Unfortunately Verchiel would do everything in his power to make certain that Lucifer never had the chance to utter those words of atonement, and would make him responsible for yet another heinous crime against God and what He holds most dear. The leader of the Powers didn't believe that Lucifer had the right to be forgiven, and there were days when he believed that Verchiel could very well be right. But it wasn't up to them to decide. God would forgive, or He wouldn't. It was simple as that—or at least it used to be.

Fight as he did, Lucifer knew he could not keep the door closed for much longer. Hell raged at his back, the pain at the core of his being, methodically peeled away like the multiple layers of an onion.

The Morningstar was ashamed, believing that he should have been stronger, able to restrain that which had been such a crucial part of him for so long. Hell had come to define him, showing what his petty jealousy and arrogance had been responsible for.

In the world of inner darkness it sounded like gunfire as the first thick metal hinge exploded from the vault door. It was followed by a second, and as he pressed his back flat against the cold surface of the door, he felt it shift within its frame. *It won't be long now,* Lucifer knew. The gaseous discharge of the accumulated misery on the other side wafted up around him. It made him see it all again, experience it as though it were happening. It was Hell incarnate.

"I'm so sorry," he cried aloud as the door fell, trapping him beneath its tremendous weight.

And that which came to be known as Hell surged out from within him, a geyser of rage, pain, sadness, and misery garnered from the most horrible event ever to befall the kingdom of God.

"So sorry."

She looks much better, Aaron thought, watching Vilma as she slept peacefully. Silently he thanked the Malakim for what he had done for her—for him—and swore that Verchiel would be made to pay for his crimes.

He reached down and pulled the blanket up over the girl. It was damp in the basement, and she had enough problems without catching a cold to boot.

"She's much better, thanks to you," Gabriel said from nearby.

Aaron couldn't stop watching her.

"You love her, don't you?"

Aaron's first impulse was to deny it; he'd never admitted it out loud before. But the fact was he did love Vilma Santiago, and as he watched her sleep, he couldn't imagine his life without her. Aaron remembered the Archon's words about his mate, and the beautiful children they would have together. Vilma was part of his future. He just hoped she wanted him to be a part of hers.

"Yep, I guess I do," he finally responded. He looked at the dog that was lying on the concrete floor not far from the foot of the mattress. "Is that cool with you?"

Gabriel was staring at Vilma as well, and Aaron could feel the emotion emanating from the Labrador's dark, soulful eyes. *"It's cool,"* he said, blinking slowly. *"She'll be good for our pack."*

Aaron smiled. "Won't she though?" he agreed, rising from her side.

"Do you have to go?" the Labrador asked, climbing to his feet as well.

Aaron nodded, knowing his options were few and time was growing slim. His father had been weakening, and who knew what kind of power Verchiel now had at his disposal. If what Lucifer told him was true, the leader of the Powers wasn't just gunning for Nephilim and fallen angels anymore; he had a score to settle with the whole planet.

"This is it, Gabe," he told the animal. "Verchiel is going down for good this time."

"My sentiments exactly," Lehash said as he walked down the stairs toward them, Scholar close behind.

Aaron had been waiting for them to arrive, certain that Lorelei would have gone to them as soon as he'd revealed his intentions.

Scholar looked pale as he maneuvered around Lehash. "Lorelei told us what you learned," he said, a tremble in his voice. "Verchiel has lost it completely. It was bad enough that he wanted *us* dead, but to intentionally unleash that kind of force upon the earth . . ." The fallen angel stopped, speechless for the first time that Aaron could recall.

Lehash's pistols flared to life in his grasp and he spun them on his fingers in true cowboy fashion. "Never met a son of a bitch that deserved two in the brain pan more," he proclaimed.

Vilma stirred at the sound of their voices, rolling onto her side before returning to the embrace of healing slumber.

"I'm doing this alone," Aaron said softly.

Lehash's heavenly weapons dispersed in a flash. "Must be the acoustics down here," the gunslinger said, sticking a finger in his ear and wiggling it around. "But I'd swear you just said you were going to face Verchiel alone."

Aaron nodded. "That's what I said."

Lehash scowled and Aaron prepared for the onslaught that he knew would be coming. "You're not going anywhere alone, boy," he snarled. "Look at you," the cowboy said, throwing out one black-gloved hand toward him. "Yer lucky you can stand, for pity's sake. You just got stuck with a spear—and almost died! This ringing any bells?"

Aaron's hand instinctively went to the bandage on his chest. The wound was still painful, but he was healing quickly, another perk of being a Nephilim. "It's not that I don't want your help. In fact nothing would make me feel safer than to have you guys at my side when this finally goes down."

Lehash studied him, slowly folding his arms across his chest while Scholar simply stared.

"But I've come to realize that I have to do this alone."

Lehash shook his head. "It ain't true," he grumbled.

"It is," Aaron answered. "This has been about me from the start. Verchiel lost it because of the prophecy." He pointed to himself. "I'm that prophecy, I'm the physical manifestation of all that he hates. It's got to be me that takes him down."

"*He almost killed you, Aaron,*" Gabriel said, his gruff animal voice filled with concern.

"Key word being 'almost,'" Aaron responded. "I wasn't ready before. I didn't understand what all this angel stuff was about. But I do now. I know how much is at stake. It's not just fallen angels and Nephilim that are in danger. It's the entire world."

Lehash rubbed his hand across the rough skin of his face. "He won't go down easy. An animal's at its most dangerous when its back is up against the wall."

"*He's right about that*," Gabriel said, fortifying the gunslinger's words.

"Believe me, I know that I could very well be killed, but I also know that it's for me to do, and me alone. *I've* got to be the one who ends this."

The room became very still, the only sound Vilma's gentle breathing as she slept.

"'And the one shall come that will bring about the end of their pain, his furious struggle building a bridge between the penitent and what has been lost,'" Scholar said, his stare vacant, as if he were looking beyond the room, perhaps into the future. "That's a line from the prophecy," he said, his eyes focused on them again. "Your prophecy."

And Aaron knew it was time to go. He reached within himself and drew upon the power of angels, feeling the names of all those who died fighting for Lucifer's cause rising to the surface to adorn his flesh. *This is for them, as well,* he thought. His senses grew more keen, the fury of Heaven thrumming in his blood. He brought forth his wings of blackest night, unfurling them slowly, fanning the air in anticipation.

"I have to go now," he said in a severe voice he had come to recognize as his own, a voice filled with strength and purpose.

He looked at them all, perhaps for the last time, and an unspoken message passed between them. This was hard enough without the hindrance of final words, and even though they would not be by his side in this last battle, they would in fact be with him in spirit, providing the strength he would need to fight.

"See you when this is done," Aaron said, Vilma's peaceful sleep his last sight before departing to fulfill his destiny.

It had never known such a connection to another living thing.

Its tiny heart beat rapidly; its respirations quickened as it listened to the furtive moans of its friend in agony.

The others of his kind were hurting him again, their droning chants making him writhe and cry out. They sat around the outside of his circle, rocking from side to side as they repeated their hurtful song.

Something leaked out from the tortured creature's body. The mouse was reminded of the morning fog on the river outside the mountain monastery that used to be its home, only that fog was not the color of dried blood and did not bring with it such feelings of unease. Something was coming into the world that did not belong, and the mouse's friend cried out in abandon, a mournful song filled with shame at not being strong enough to prevent it.

The one called Verchiel impatiently paced before the hanging figure, his gaze fixed upon the tortured one. It was he who was behind it all, he who was responsible for all the pain.

The rodent could not bear to hear it any longer, did not want its friend to think that he suffered alone, and against all instincts it scampered across the wooden floor, no longer caring if it was seen or not. The mouse passed between two of the chanting ones, reaching the ring of foul smelling dirt. It stifled the frenzied urges to flee, its tiny eyes fixed upon the face of the one called friend. It had but one purpose now.

The dirt on the floor was cold and damp and stank of death, but it did not hinder the mouse as it forced its way through the mire, interrupting the perfection of the circle's curve. It had broken the circle and the patterns beyond, without notice, conquering its fear and reaching its friend.

Standing upon its hind legs, the mouse raised its pointed face and reached up with its two front paws to the sad figure hanging above it. *"You are not alone,"* it squeaked in the most rudimentary of languages.

Triumphant, yet unaware of what it had truly done.

Verchiel was mesmerized by Lucifer's suffering.

He could not pull his gaze away, watching as the greatest of sinners strained to keep God's punishment within him.

"Let it go, damn you," Verchiel hissed, the anticipation almost more than he could bear.

Soon they will all pay, the angel thought with a perverse sense of satisfaction—the human monkeys scurrying about thinking themselves so much more, the fallen angels and their Nephilim spawn, and the Lord God. *How sad that it has come to this,* the Powers commander ruminated as he watched the first of the fallen writhe. Verchiel was surprised that one such as Lucifer could care so much for the primitive world to which he had been banished. He himself could no longer hide his distaste for the place and its corrupting influence over his Father in Heaven.

"I shall show You the error of Your ways," he spoke aloud, hoping that the Almighty would hear his words and know how wrong He had been to discard him. Verchiel would show the Creator the madness of it all.

Suddenly Lucifer, the first of the fallen, let loose a scream that spoke of his final resignation. The collected horror that was his punishment flowed from his body, pouring from the opening cut into his chest—a thick, undulating vapor eager to make the acquaintance of the world.

"How utterly horrible you are," Verchiel whispered with a kind of twisted admiration, moving closer to the magickal circle that acted as the punishment's cage. "What terror you shall reap under my command."

He looked about the room at the last of his

soldiers, bloody and beaten by a crusade gone to seed. Once they had numbered in the hundreds, but now less then twenty remained under his command. And once they would have fought hard against a threat such as this, not unlocked its cage to set it free upon a thankless world. The angels fluttered their wings nervously, sensing the fearsome virility of the power that was being unleashed. They remembered it—the war—and what it had done to them all, the scars it had left.

"Do not fear, my brothers," Verchiel proclaimed, "for with this force we shall be vindicated, and every living thing, whether of flesh and blood or of the divine, will know that our mission was righteous, and will beg for our forgiveness."

The Archons began to scream, and Verchiel looked toward the angelic magicians. Somehow the power leaking from Lucifer's body had managed to break free of its containment, moving past the mystical circle of Heaven's soil and his adversary's blood, swirling around his faithful sorcerers like a swarm of insects. The Archons' screams were frantic, unlike anything he had ever heard before.

Archon Oraios ran toward the Powers commander, his head enshrouded in a shifting cloud that clung stubbornly like a thing alive. "How could we have been so foolish!" the magician wailed, arms flailing in panic. "To think that we had the right—to think that we could erase His Word!"

Verchiel grabbed the angel by his robes as he passed, throwing him violently to the gymnasium floor, and still the cloud remained. A sword of fire came to life in the commander's grasp. "What is happening here?" he spat, watching as the punishment of God continued to leak from Lucifer's body, past the circle of containment, and into the room.

"It's loose," Oraios cried, thrashing upon the floor as the cloud expanded to engulf the magician's body. "Somehow the circle was broken and now it is free. How could we have been so stupid as to think we could control it!"

The gymnasium erupted in a cacophony of screams and moans as the Lord's punishment acquainted itself with the others in the room. Verchiel watched aghast as warriors he had fought beside in the most horrendous of battles were reduced to mewling animals. They cowered in the scarlet cloud—the embodiment of all the suffering caused by the war in Heaven. It laid waste to them all, driving them to destroy themselves. One tore out his eyes, while others turned their own fiery weapons upon themselves. Their screams were deafening.

"You must do something," Verchiel barked at the Archons as an angel of the Powers host repeatedly flew into one of the room's concrete walls, as if trying to shatter all the bones in its body.

The three Archons crowded together in the

far corner of the gymnasium, trying to hide from the force they had unleashed.

"Do something!" Verchiel screamed again, but they only huddled closer, trembling violently.

"They're afraid," said a voice, little more than a whisper.

Verchiel looked to see that Lucifer was awake, even as the power continued to leak from his body. "*You* did this," Verchiel said with a snarl, pointing his fiery sword at the prisoner. "*You* caused this to go awry."

Another of the Powers host took his own life, his mournful wails reverberating horribly off the cold walls before falling silent.

Lucifer laughed painfully, the rumbling chuckle turning into a wet, hacking cough. "I'm the one hanging over a mystical circle with his chest cut open, and this is my fault," he said in wonder. "How is that?"

Suddenly Verchiel caught movement from within the circle's center and noticed the prisoner's pet vermin, cleaning dirt and blood from its dirtied stomach. He was about to snatch up the bothersome creature and squeeze the life from its body, but then he realized that it wouldn't matter.

There was a sudden searing flash of heat and Verchiel looked back to see that the Archons had set themselves ablaze. He could hear their voices raised in unison as the mystical fire consumed them, begging the Creator for forgiveness. They remained alive far longer than he would have imagined possible, before their piteous pleas ceased and they collapsed to the wood floor in a pile of fiery ash and oily black smoke.

"Set me free," Lucifer said as Verchiel returned his attentions to his prisoner. "Do the right thing. Redeem yourself. Let me reclaim my punishment. Let me put it back where it belongs," the first of the fallen pleaded. "There's a chance we might still be able to stop this."

Verchiel gazed out over the gymnasium where the broken, bleeding forms of his remaining followers littered the floor. The cloud of misery was expanding, rolling inexorably toward him. It had finished with his soldiers and now wished to feast upon their leader. He tensed, waiting for its dreadful touch with a strange anticipation.

"Who said anything about wanting to stop it?" Verchiel replied as he was engulfed in the hungry red mist. He felt it cling to his body, worming its way inside him through the open wounds that adorned his flesh. He waited to feel the unrelenting horrors of the Almighty's punishment, but instead felt the same ever-present sense of rage he'd had since being abandoned by God.

And then the leader of the Powers came to a startling realization. *I'm already living the torments of Hell.*

chapter fourteen

$\mathcal{I}$n his mind Aaron saw his destination, a barely legible, weather-beaten sign that read SAINT ATHANASIUS CHURCH AND ORPHANAGE: ESTABLISHED 1899. This was where the final battle would occur. There were multiple buildings, including a church, but he knew he needed to be inside the school. That was where his father was being held. That was the image Lucifer had placed within the Nephilim's mind.

The picture of the gymnasium inside his head made him think briefly of his own school, Kenneth Curtis High, and all he had given up—graduation, college, a human life. He had been so angry in the beginning, that his once normal life had been turned on its head by angelic prophecies and blood-thirsty angels, circumstances beyond his control, a destiny he had known nothing about. And even though time had allowed him a begrudging acceptance of his fate, it hadn't made his sacrifices any less difficult.

He parted his wings like the curtains on a stage pulled back to present the last act of some great production. *This is it*, he thought in nervous anticipation, the final chapter of a story that began on the morning of his eighteenth birthday, the day his life changed forever.

He furled his great black wings beneath the flesh of his back, their movement stirring a strange, reddish fog that drifted above the floor of the gymnasium. An atmosphere of danger permeated the room, and the hair at the back of his neck prickled, a sword of fire springing to life in his hand. He was ready for this to end.

His eyes scanned his surroundings. The mist was thick, but he was able to make out the features of the old gymnasium, the hard parquet floor covered with years of dust beneath his feet, a skylight in the ceiling above, spattered with bird droppings. He moved his hand through the dense vapor, wondering what it was, knowing it couldn't be good. It made the bare flesh of his arms tingle, his chest ache as he reluctantly took it into his lungs.

Then it hit him with the force of a storm driven wave. His weapon of fire fell from his grasp as his body was wracked with violent spasms. *What's happening?* Aaron wondered on the brink of panic as the synapses in his brain exploded like fireworks on the Fourth of July. It was as if every emotion—rage, despair, love, joy—had come alive at once, more incapacitating than any physical attack. He was numb, stumbling through the billowing red fog, trying to regain control of his runaway passions. He had no doubt now as to what this was. He was too late. His father's curse had been unleashed.

The punishment of God was free.

Try as he might, Aaron could not wrest control of his emotions. The mist cajoled them, inflamed them, drawing them out like infection from a wound. Raw, unhindered feelings that ran the gamut from sadness to rage to joy were released within him. Again and again he lived the moments that had created them, the mundane and the profound, the joyous and the miserable.

Fear flashed through him as he saw the first foster home he could truly remember, horrible people who had taken him in only for the meager allowance the state paid for his upkeep. He felt the loneliness and anger, relived the abuse and neglect. Then that experience was viciously torn away to be replaced with another, and then another still. It was as if all the defining emotional moments of his life were happening simultaneously: the early endless stream of foster homes, the fights at school, his discovery of Gabriel—a filthy puppy tied to a tree in a gang member's backyard—the first time he saw Vilma

Santiago, and the deaths of the Stanleys, the only true parents he ever knew.

Aaron tried to block them out, to hold them at bay, but the experiences were relentless, an assault upon his every sense. His confusion turned to rage, and then to panic. He lashed out with a newly summoned blade of fire, futilely cutting through the swirling crimson vapor, doing anything to fight back, but to no avail.

The fog grew thicker, hungrily closing in around him. And suddenly, as if his own emotional turmoil hadn't been enough, every aspect of the war in Heaven bombarded his already torn and frayed senses. He saw the crystal spires of Heaven stained crimson with the blood of discord, smelled the sickly sweet aroma of burning angel flesh, and listened to the cries of brothers, once comrades in the glory that was Heaven, locked in furious combat. *How easily it all fell apart*, he sadly observed as he experienced the woe of God, a despair the likes of which he could not even begin to describe. It was all encompassing, a sucking void that pulled him in and devoured all hope.

At that devastating moment Aaron fully understood the magnitude of his father's crimes and the fallout that followed. To go against the Creator, to strike at God—it was the pinnacle of sin, the saddest of all things. He could think of no way to escape the anguish of it. The malaise was like an enormous hand pushing him down to the ground, crushing him, and he came to the sickening realization that nothing mattered, that the struggle of the fallen angels for forgiveness was to no avail.

It was hopeless.

All his sacrifice and struggle had been for naught.

With a trembling hand Aaron brought his weapon of fire to his throat and prepared to end it—to make the misery stop. He felt the searing bite of the blade's flaming edge upon the flesh of his neck, but did not pull away. It was a blessed relief to feel something other than the sorrow of the Lord God.

"*Stop*," begged a voice riding upon the churning mist of crimson.

And strangely it stayed his hand, the fiery blade faltering. Aaron stumbled through the unnatural fog, stepping over the bodies of others who had released themselves from the pain of Heaven's fall, drawn toward the voice, an island of hope in a sea of desperation.

The image of a man hanging from the ceiling in chains appeared in the roiling vapor. Aaron moved closer and could see the glowing, archaic symbols etched upon the dark metal restraints, symbols infused with the ability to sap away the strength of the angelic.

He reached up to help the man down as further waves of drowning emotion washed over him, and he again found himself contemplating his sword. *It'll be quick and relatively painless*, he thought, raising the blade of fire to his throat. *Anything to take away the hurt . . .*

"That's not the way," the hanging man croaked, and raised his head of curly black hair to look upon Aaron with eyes deep and dark, old eyes filled with centuries of pain.

Aaron knew this man, so long associated with all that was evil and wrong with the world. He was pulled into Lucifer's gaze, unexpectedly feeling as though he had been tossed a life preserver, adrift in a furious sea of rabid sensation. "It . . . it hurts so much," he said, clutching a prized moment of solace, fearing he would not have the strength to endure the next pummeling wave.

"But think about how good it will feel when it stops," Lucifer whispered, his head slowly falling forward again.

The red cloud churned around the fallen angel, emanating from a gaping, vertical wound that began in the center of his chest, the horrible gash splayed open with metal clamps. Aaron was reminded of the cat he'd had to dissect in his junior year biology class, only this subject was somehow still alive.

"You've got to use it," Lucifer murmured. "The pain. Use it as fuel to move past the torment, to the light at the end of the tunnel—punishment to absolution. It's what's kept me relatively sane since the Fall." He strained to smile. "It's good to see you in person, son. Only wish the circumstances were a bit less hairy."

Aaron moved closer to the prisoner, fighting to keep his feelings in check. "Let me help you," he said, preparing to use his heavenly blade to sever the debilitating chains and release the fallen angel that was his father.

Lucifer's head rose. "Watch your back," he croaked in warning, and Aaron spun around, his sword instinctively raised, blocking another weapon of fire as it descended out of the mist to end his life.

"You'll do no such thing," Verchiel screamed, emerging from the deadly fog.

Aaron was momentarily shocked by the angel's decaying appearance. The heavenly armor that once gleamed like the sun was now dirty gray. The usually firm and modeled flesh of his arms and legs was wrapped haphazardly in blood-stained bandages. His face was like a single, open wound.

Their weapons hissed as they bit into one another, shrapnel of heavenly fire cutting through the air. Aaron cried out in sudden pain, his cheek glanced by the sword's fiery embers.

"The end is upon us," the leader of the Powers rumbled as he bore down upon his weapon, attempting to drive Aaron to his knees.

"That's probably the first and last time I'll ever agree with you, you son of a bitch," Aaron snarled, calling forth his wings, pushing forward, driving his attacker back, using the rabid emotions as his father ordered.

The two angelic entities glided across the gym, locked in a furious struggle, the Creator's punishment flowing around them, becoming darker, thicker, as if egging them on. It was taking all that Aaron had to ignore the multitude of emotions that made him want to drop his sword, to give in to the sadness and despair all around them. He raged against the disparaging feelings, reminding himself of all those who were depending on him.

Verchiel pressed his attack, his sword coming dangerously close to severing Aaron's head from his shoulders. The Nephilim flapped his powerful wings, sending himself up toward the muted light from the skylight, Verchiel in heated pursuit. Then he suddenly spun around, arcing downward, plowing into the angel and sending them both plummeting to the gymnasium floor.

They hit the hard wood with incredible force, boards splintering and popping from the impact. Verchiel shrieked, thrashing beneath him. He reached up and dragged a clawed hand across Aaron's face, barely missing his eyes. The Nephilim leaped away and noticed that he was covered in blood. It took him but a heartbeat to realize that it was not his own, but Verchiel's. The injuries beneath the angel's bandages were bleeding profusely and he stank of rot.

Verchiel climbed to his feet, his great wings

flexed, feathers shedding like falling leaves. He glanced down upon himself, the blood from his injuries running down his body in rivulets to pool at his feet. "This is what it's come to," the Powers leader said, a despair in his voice that only added to the anguish roiling about them. "It's all been taken away from me." He glared at Aaron with black, hate-filled eyes. "*You've* taken it away from me—you and the monster that spawned you."

"Do you honestly believe that we're entirely to blame?" Aaron stared hard at the angel, his gaze unwavering. "That we've somehow pulled one over on God, and you're the only one who knows about it?" He shook his head in disgust. "What a load of crap."

Verchiel seethed, fists clenched before him, black blood oozing between his fingers to patter like gentle rain upon the floor.

"Sins were committed," Aaron continued. "Crimes so unimaginable that they could never be forgiven. Or can they?"

The fog swirled about Verchiel, as if somehow attempting to comfort him. "You know nothing of what we experienced," he growled.

Aaron extended his bloodstained arms, showing the Powers leader the black sigils that adorned his flesh. "But that's where you're wrong," he said. "I wear their names, those who died fighting for Lucifer's cause. And inside of me lives a piece of each and every one of them."

The angel's horrible face twisted in revulsion. "You're more of a monstrosity than I thought," he snarled with disgust.

"A monstrosity who knows their jealousy," Aaron countered. "That feels what it was like when God seemed to turn away from them to embrace another creation on a new world. I know how desperate they were to regain his favor. Desperate enough to do something foolish."

Vechiel glanced down at the blood pooling at his feet. "They broke His holy trust and for that they deserved a punishment most severe." He looked back to Aaron. "I was doing what I was told to do. It was my holy mission to bring them down."

"The fallen eventually realized that they were wrong, but have you?" Aaron asked. "If God told you, right now, that they were to be given a chance to do penance—to prove they were truly sorry—would you even be able to hear Him?"

"I followed my commands."

"Exactly," Aaron agreed with a slight nod. "You followed *your* commands."

Verchiel turned suddenly, stalking away from him. "I'm tired of all this . . . living," he said.

Aaron noticed that one of the angel's blood-covered hands had begun to glow, and he readied himself for the next round of conflict. "Then let's see what I can do about putting you out of your misery," he replied, sword of heavenly fire burning righteously in his grasp.

The leader of the Powers turned, his right hand glowing with incredible heat, the blood running down from the wounds upon his arms, hissing snakelike, evaporating to smoke before it could drip upon the white-hot hand. He laughed, a sound void of any humor. "I wonder if He's listening now?" He turned his eyes toward the heavens and raised his burning hand. A tendril of living flame erupted to explode through the skylight and illuminate the night beyond it with the glow of Heaven's fire.

"What is that disparaging statement humans often make to each other?" the angel asked, as jagged pieces of the broken glass rained down upon him. "Go to Hell?"

And Aaron realized what was happening. He watched in stunned horror as the crimson mist coalesced, snaking across the floor like some prehistoric serpent, over the bodies of those felled by its malignant touch, eager to invade the world beyond these walls.

"Yes, that's right," Verchiel said with an obvious glee. "You can all go to Hell."

Kraus tried to squeeze himself deeper into the darkened corner of an abandoned classroom, a cacophony of emotions bringing him to the brink of insanity. All the anguish, anger, and loneliness that had been part of his early life was with him again, the intensified feelings bombarding him threefold.

With his new eyes he had watched the angelic ritual performed upon the fallen angel Lucifer. Even before the last of the rite was completed, the healer knew that nothing good would come from it, and he attempted to hide himself away.

For decades he had served the angelic host Powers, developing a certain preternatural sense for things beyond the norm. As most humans were oblivious to the paranormal, Kraus found that he had become keenly sensitive. Those senses were screaming now, and he attempted to fold himself tighter into a ball, to protect himself from the forces that had been turned loose this day.

How could I have been so blind?

Though a force from Heaven, Verchiel had become twisted, obsessed with the completion of his holy charge no matter how high the cost. And Kraus had helped him. How strange it was that it took the leader of the Powers host rewarding him with the gift of sight for him to truly see how things actually were.

I was blind, but now I can see.

Kraus heard the cries of his classmates at the Perry School as they were consumed by fire, and he shuddered in the darkness. There had been no act of mercy that fateful night, only murder.

He was suddenly reminded of something

Lucifer had said to him only days ago, and fought an unrelenting wave of fear to remember exactly what had been said. The healer had found himself drawn to the prisoner's cage, although he had been instructed never to enter the room in which the Powers' captive had been imprisoned. Somehow he sensed that he was needed, that his skills as a healer were being called for. Still condemned to darkness, he had gathered his instruments and healing potions, feeling his way to the schoolroom where the personification of all that was evil was imprisoned.

Evil personified. Kraus would have laughed if he weren't so afraid.

The Devil had welcomed him into the room, and Kraus stood strong against him. He knew he had to be on guard, for the prisoner's manipulative ways were legendary. He had bravely informed the prisoner that he was a healer and had come only to administer to the fallen angel's wounds. Lucifer had said he understood, and although most of his burns had healed, he wished for Kraus to treat a few stubborn patches.

The healer had stoically obliged. It was his duty, after all, to care for the angelic creatures around him, whether they were soldier or prisoner. But he found himself in awe of this prisoner's demeaner. Here was the Prince of Darkness, the Lord of Lies, imprisoned by the forces of Good, and all he could talk about was how much he enjoyed the springtime, and could he please have some bread for his friend, a mouse.

Was it then that the first seeds of doubt were planted? Kraus wondered. Or had it been with those final words, as he completed the application of healing salve upon Lucifer's burns?

"It's going to get worse around here before it can get better," Lucifer had warned. *"That's the way it has to be, but I thought you might want to know."*

He had wanted to ask the prisoner to explain, for he had already begun to suspect, to feel, that the near future was ripe with the potential for danger. The words were at the tip of his tongue, ready to fall from his mouth, when Verchiel returned from his latest defeat at the hands of the Nephilim. He had been lucky that the Powers commander hadn't slain him then and there, but the angel had been preoccupied with his plans for the future and Kraus had quickly fled.

The future.

Lucifer's words again echoed through his mind. *"It's going to get worse around here before it can get better."*

Kraus uncurled himself and leaned back against the cold plaster wall. He remembered the last time he had seen the prisoner, hanging from the ceiling in chains, his torso cut open and something unspeakable leaking out into the world.

"Very bad indeed," he muttered, afraid to

move, afraid to incite another pummeling wave of the supernatural force that seemed to have subsided for the moment, allowing him to gather his wits about him.

"Why would he have told me that?" Kraus asked the oppressive gloom.

In his mind he saw the mist leaking from Lucifer's wound—saw how he fought to keep it inside—and Kraus knew he had to do something.

The thought of leaving his hiding place filled him with mortal terror. What was happening beyond the walls of this classroom was not meant to be seen by mere man. And besides, what could he possibly do to prevent it?

"That's the way it has to be."

Kraus finally found the strength within himself to stand, and before he could question the sanity of his actions, went to the door.

"But I thought you might want to know."

He moved through the darkened school, the eerie vapor that had once been contained within the first of the fallen becoming thicker as he neared the gymnasium. Kraus tried with all his might not to let it affect him, not to be reduced to quivering human wreckage by its touch. It was the hardest thing he had ever done, plunging headlong into that debilitating mist. He waited for it to overcome him, to crush him beneath the overpowering weight of its despair, but it did not happen. *Perhaps more than the ability to see was bestowed upon me by Verchiel's restorative touch,* Kraus considered.

It was like being blind again as he felt his way through the swirling mist, stumbling over the bodies of those who had already fallen victim to the full extent of the vapor's malignancy. He could not bring himself to look at them, for they had been his charges for decades, their well-being his responsibility, and it hurt him deeply to know that there was nothing he could have done to ease their pain.

A limp human shape, hanging from the ceiling's metal girders by thick links of metal chain, loomed out of the drifting mist before him. But now that he had reached his goal, Kraus was unsure of why exactly he had come. He could hear sounds within the fog, voices raised in rage, and he suspected that the Nephilim had come to challenge Verchiel's insanity.

"It's bad," Kraus muttered to the unconscious figure, clutching his satchel of healing tools to his chest as if they could somehow protect him. The deafening sound of an explosion and the shattering of glass made the healer wince, and he shielded his head from possible hurt. "Very bad," he whispered, and he felt the cool touch of the fresh night air invade the stagnant atmosphere of the gym.

He noticed that the mist was being drawn toward an opening in the ceiling where a skylight had been, and the nightmarish images of the vapor expanding across the globe filled his head. "I can't imagine it any worse," Kraus muttered.

And Lucifer slowly raised his head.

"Help me down," he said. "I think that's my cue."

Aaron watched in terror as Verchiel rose up alongside the integrated fog, wings beating the air as he followed the seething mass on its undulating course toward the open skylight, toward its freedom.

Then instinct took over and Aaron spread his wings and leaped into the air. The manifestation of Heaven's grief had become something akin to a single great tentacle, slithering through the air pointed at the gaping hole in the ceiling.

"You have to stop this!" he screamed at Verchiel, his blade of fire passing uselessly through the gaseous mass. At one time the Powers leader must have been a rational thinking being, and he hoped to somehow appeal to what remained of that creature, if anything remained at all. "You claim to be a loyal servant of God, and yet you're going to allow this to happen? Think about what you're doing!"

Verchiel hovered just below the shattered framework of the skylight, his tattered wings flapping furiously to keep his form aloft. His dark, horrible eyes were riveted to the snake of fog. Night had fallen outside, and despite the horror of what was happening below, the stars in the sky twinkled beautifully. If the mist were allowed to escape, Aaron wondered if the night sky would ever look this beautiful again.

"He has to be shown," Verchiel said dreamily, beckoning for the deadly vapor to flow all the faster. "If I'd only been allowed to complete my mission, this never would have happened." He shook his head sadly as if there was nothing more that he could do. "It is too late—too late for us all."

Aaron flew at the Powers commander, thoughts racing. There had to something he could do to stop it. Anything. "It'll be the death of us *all*!" he shouted at the angel, desperately trying to reach any hint of the divine still lurking within Verchiel. He had turned this monstrous haze on; he had to know how to shut it off.

The leader of the Powers brought forth his own sword of fire, swiping at Aaron, driving him back. "Yes, it will be our death!" he cried out, his face a blood-covered mask of open sores, "and *He* will be forced to bear that guilt."

Aaron narrowly avoided the bite of Verchiel's burning blade, riding dangerously close to the hellish mass. The angel came at him again, his bandaged hand closing about the Nephilim's throat, forcing him back into the punishment of God.

Aaron struggled violently to be free, but Verchiel's grip was like steel. He felt as though he were drowning, every fiber of his being invaded by the experience that was the War in Heaven. Finally he managed to break away, falling toward the ground, unable to function— barely able to cope with what his body was experiencing. He landed with a sickening thud and painfully rolled over on his back, looking up at the ceiling. He thought of the world beyond the gym. He had seen what Lucifer's hell had done to the angelic, heavenly beings of amazing power and strength, and shuddered to think of the horrors that would soon befall the people of the world.

Struggling to collect himself, Aaron yelled at the angel hovering near the ceiling above him. "You have to stop it!"

Verchiel simply smiled, the marble pale skin of his face hidden in blood. "I can't," he said with a shake of his head. And his smile grew all the larger and twice as terrible.

Verchiel recognized some of the misery emanating from the body of the condensed vapor as his own. Anger turning to rage, sadness to overwhelming despair; all of them he had experienced during the Morningstar's war in Heaven and during his own recent abandoment. He had contributed mightily to this swirling miasma of experience, and now it was to be released upon the world.

The angel's black eyes gazed up through the

open ceiling from which Hell would escape, through the cold light of stars above, and attempted to see Paradise. He had always imagined that his mission, his private war, would eventually end and that he would return to Heaven a hero of the cause. Things would be as they had been: chaos squelched, order restored, and the memory of Lucifer Morningstar and his atrocities purged from the memories of all divine beings. Verchiel saw himself basking in the celestial light of his Lord and Heavenly Father, the favored child of God, and all was right in Heaven and the universe.

But it's not meant to be, the angel forlornly reminded himself, averting his gaze from the wide sky above to the snakelike monstrosity writhing in the air below him. Here was the personification of his *own* rage, his way of punishing all those who had hurt him. A horrible but necessary way to make things right again.

The Morningstar had not been forgotten. His presence had continued to infect the heavenly domain like some malignant growth, blossoming into the cancerous prophecy of forgiveness, and eventually the state in which Verchiel currently found the world. He could take it no more; the denigration had to be stopped.

"Are you watching, my Lord?" he called to the open space above him. The stars winked as if in response. "You may have been able to forgive them their trespasses, but I cannot."

He soared up and out through the damaged skylight into the night, gazing down as the probing tip of the gaseous appendage cautiously reached beyond the skylight into the cool night air.

"That's it," the angel encouraged, a perverse satisfaction the likes of which he had never known empowering his decaying form. "This world of sin belongs to you now. Let them feel what we felt—how horribly we suffered for His love."

Verchiel looked out over central Massachusetts, his gaze traversing beyond New England to look upon the whole planet of man. "Will You forgive *me*, Heavenly Father?" he whispered. "When *my* sin is committed and my penance is done, will You take *me* back into Your embrace?"

He again looked upon the monstrous thing that had been the bane of Lucifer as it prepared to make its way into the world.

But something was wrong.

It hesitated.

Verchiel flew closer and watched in surprise as the hellish mass began to recede into the building. "Come back!" he roared pitifully, his cries of disappointment echoing through the still of the night.

He descended, following the serpentine form back into the building, Bringer of Sorrow ignited in his grasp.

There was Lucifer Morningstar kneeling

upon the floor of the gymnasium, his own fingers now holding open the gaping wound in his chest, an expression of unadulterated suffering etched upon his features, as he gradually drew the thick crimson vapor back within himself. Standing beside him, a supportive hand upon the first of the fallen's bare shoulder, stood Verchiel's own healer, the monkey Kraus.

"What is this?" the angel growled aghast, not so much that the Morningstar was free, but that one who had served him so faithfully, on whom he bestowed such a great gift, could be party to Verchiel's own betrayal.

"I'm taking it back," Lucifer said, struggling to his feet with the help of the human animal. "It is not the world's burden." The enormous volume of swirling mist slowly burrowed back inside his body. "It is my punishment. I am its master, and it is mine alone to bear."

"You always were a selfish one, Lucifer Morningstar," Verchiel ranted as he dropped from the ceiling, placing all his might behind what would be a killing blow.

chapter fifteen

$\mathfrak{T}$ime slowed as Verchiel's blade fell toward him.

For a glorious few moments Lucifer had experienced what it was like to be free of his burden. It had been bliss, and for an instant he considered the possibility of life again without his punishment.

I've done more than enough penance, he thought, trying to convince himself that it wouldn't be such a bad thing to let God's chastening of him go. *I'm truly sorry for all my sins. He must know that,* Lucifer rationalized. *Maybe this is how it was supposed to be. Is this how I'm to be freed from the Lord's wrath?*

He looked up now and saw Verchiel above him, armor tarnished, skin covered in tattered, blood-stained bandages and open sores, decaying wings spread wide as he fell toward him, hissing weapon of fire falling toward his face. *Is this a messenger from God?* Lucifer asked himself. *One that the Creator sent to tell me I am forgiven?* But no matter how hard he tried to convince himself, Lucifer knew the answer.

It was not yet his time for absolution.

Wearily he began to take it back, all the pain, sorrow, anger, and misery spawned by his jealousy. The chore was daunting and excruciating, and the first of the fallen wasn't sure he had the strength left to finish it. But the human healer, Kraus, had lent him some of his own strength, and Lucifer had managed to complete his task.

Hell churned inside him again. It belonged to him and nobody else. It would be his until the day he was forgiven, or his life was brought to an end.

And not before.

Which brought him back to the here and now. Verchiel's blade was dangerously close. Lucifer thought of conjuring his own weapon of choice, a fiery trident that could have easily challenged Verchiel's blade of sorrow. But in his millenia on Earth he had developed an aversion to violence, and it had been so long since he last summoned a weapon from Heaven's arsenal. The image of the three-pronged weapon began to form in his mind.

He was not as fast as he once was, and he could feel the heat of Verchiel's blade upon his face as sparks of heavenly fire filled his hands. Hopefully he would not be too slow. It would be sad to have come this far only to die now.

Although he had difficulty with the details, the trident began to take shape and Lucifer raised his arm. The weapon wasn't quite ready, and he feared that it would not have enough substance to prevent the sword of sorrow from cleaving his skull, but there was no time left. He had to try. He pushed Kraus away, out of harm's reach, and prepared to meet Verchiel's attack.

Bringer of Sorrow cut through Lucifer's weapon as if it were not there, and the first of the fallen readied for the blade's searing bite. He was sorry that it had come to this, sorry that he hadn't more time to spend with his son, sorry that he hadn't been forgiven. Then it stopped less than an inch from his nose, an equally impressive blade of Heaven blocking Verchiel's strike with a resounding crackle of divine fire.

Lucifer turned to see his son in all his Nephilim glory, wings of raven black, body adorned with the names of those who had sworn allegiance to the Morningstar and died for his cause. He certainly was a sight to behold.

"Thank you," Lucifer said with a sigh of relief.

"*De nada,*" Aaron replied before turning his full attention to the Powers commander.

"Let's finish this," the Nephilim said impatiently, and the angel Verchiel appeared eager to oblige.

Blades still touching, opposing forces sputtering and sparking angrily, Aaron placed himself between Verchiel and Lucifer Morningstar. It was his turn now.

He remembered the first time he had seen the angelic creature that would unmercifully steal away so much that was important to him, immaculately dressed in his dark suit and trench coat, gliding into his foster parents' house on Baker Street as if he belonged there. *He actually believed that what he was doing was right,* Aaron thought bitterly. Killing his parents, burning down their home, and kidnapping his little brother. *Oh yes, that was exactly what God wanted, for sure.*

The sight before Aaron now was nothing short of pathetic—filthy, blood-covered, and ragged—but no less dangerous. He thought of asking the creature to give up, providing him with a chance to put away his sword and stop the inevitable, but he knew it wouldn't happen.

"So, we going to do this?" Aaron asked, his steely gaze unwavering.

Verchiel spat upon the floor, a thick, bloody phlegm that, by the sound of it, was filled with teeth. "Oh yessss," he hissed as he wiped his mouth with the back of a bandaged hand, and attacked.

Aaron parried his assault and followed through with one of his own, driving the last of the Powers away from the still recovering Morningstar. *It's like fighting a wild animal,* he thought, the angel growling and spitting with each opposing move as they hacked and slashed at each other across the gymnasium floor.

Aaron's back struck up against the cool concrete wall and he managed to duck as Verchiel's blade cut across its surface, leaving a deep, smoldering furrow in the building stone. The angel moved in to strike again and the boy saw his opportunity, a memory of countless fights while growing up. Using his wings, he propelled himself forward and slammed his fist into the face of his foe. It was like hitting melting ice, wet, on the verge of yielding, but not yet ready to crumble. Verchiel flipped backward, wings flapping wildly as he landed on the floor.

Certain that at least two of his knuckles had been broken, Aaron shook the pain from his hand. "That was for Doctor Jonas," he said, remembering his psychiatrist, the first victim of the Powers' hunt for him.

Verchiel's face was a bloody mess, a combination of blood and teeth oozing from his swollen mouth as he rolled to his knees, beginning to rise. Anger flared in Aaron and he surged toward the angel again, preparing to deliver a powerful kick to his side.

The Powers commander caught his leg,

twisting it savagely to one side, and Aaron fell to the floor. The angel scrambled across the floor toward him, a horrific, blood-stained sight, the insane jagged grin of a jack-o'-lantern on his once pristine features.

The Nephilim lashed out with the heel of his shoe, connecting with the side of the angel's face. It did little to slow him down as he scrabbled atop Aaron, wings flapping, long, spidery fingers winding about his throat and beginning to squeeze.

"I've longed for this moment, *monster*," Verchiel gurgled, bloody saliva dripping from his injured mouth and running down Aaron's face. "To kill you with my bare hands, to watch the accursed life leave your eyes."

Vibrant blossoms of color exploded before Aaron's eyes as the angel's viselike grip grew tighter. Instinctively a weapon of fire began to form in his hand, but he couldn't concentrate, the images in his head a jumbled mess. Darkness began to creep in around the edges of his vision. He thought of a knife, a simple thing made for only one purpose.

With failing strength he drove the blade into Verchiel's side. The tip of the knife deflected off the angel's armored chest plate, sparks of fire exploding between them, but it was enough to distract his foe, and his grip loosened. Aaron managed to pull a knee up beneath his attacker, and with the last of his reserves, he flipped

Verchiel over and behind him. He flexed his wings and sprung up from the floor, whirling around as the burning knife grew into a sword of fire.

Verchiel was already up on his feet, charging, Bringer of Sorrow held aloft in both hands. "The prophecy dies with you, Nephilim!" he screamed as he brought the blade down upon Aaron. "I can be satisfied with that victory alone."

The force of the blow was devastating, driving Aaron to his knees as he blocked the blazing sword's descent. "Hate to disappoint you," he snarled as he leaped to his feet, pushing Verchiel away with his sword, "but the only victory today is for the fallen angels, when I put you down once and for *all*." He could feel the strength of the angel warriors whose names adorned his flesh surge through his body. Never had he felt so sure of anything as he did at that moment, perfectly attuned to what he was and what he was supposed to do.

Verchiel attacked again, his sword of heavenly fire dropping again and again as it attempted to cut him down, but his blade did not—could not—touch the Nephilim. It was as if Aaron was anticipating the Powers commander's every move, countering each parry with one of his own. Verchiel's attacks became more wild, more frenzied, but still the Nephilim did not fall.

His patience waning, Aaron finally lashed out on his own, swatting Verchiel's weapon from his hand. The angel snarled, summoning yet another instrument of death, but Aaron responded in a similar fashion, disarming the angel commander with perverse ease.

"It's done," he said, his voice filled with confidence.

Suddenly the angel warrior seemed to wilt before his eyes, as if the fight had finally been stolen from him. Verchiel dropped to one knee, his head bowed.

"Do it," he spat, refusing to look at the Nephilim.

Aaron clutched the hilt of his own blade all the tighter, feeling the heat of his weapon course through his arm. The warrior's essence housed inside him screamed in rage. Here was his enemy kneeling before him in supplication, an enemy that had taken away so much, and still he stayed his hand. If he were to strike at Verchiel now, it would be no better than murder.

Verchiel raised his swollen, blood-covered face to fix him in the most horrible stare. "Kill me now," he demanded.

Though Aaron wanted to raise his blade and cut the monster's head in two, he restrained himself. "I may be an abomination in your eyes," he said, "but I am not a murderer."

Verchiel moved like lightning, surging up from the ground, a knife of fire in his grasp.

"Mercy from my most hated foe," he hissed serpentlike, lashing out at Aaron's exposed throat. "It would have hurt me less if you had taken my head from my shoulders."

Aaron blocked with his hand, the knife slicing through his palm rather than his throat. He jumped away from the enraged angel.

Verchiel swayed upon his feet, knife of fire still clutched in his hand, but he did not attack again. "This is far from over." He spread his wings and soared toward the open skylight. "Perhaps another time," he called as he escaped into the night with the flapping of mighty wings and a snowfall of molted feathers.

Aaron knew what he had to do.

"Be careful," he heard a voice say from across the gym, and he saw that his father was watching. The human healer knelt by his side and was stitching closed the vertical wound in his chest with a rather large needle and what looked to be thread spun from gold. "We've got quite a bit to discuss when this is all over," Lucifer said.

Aaron nodded as he spread his wings for flight. "We certainly do." Then he soared through the hole in the ceiling, in pursuit of the angel Verchiel.

The night air was cool upon his skin, a kind of balm to his injured hand, and it reinvigorated his senses, clearing his head as his eyes perused the evening sky in search of his prey.

He can't have gone far, Aaron mused. *Wouldn't have gone far. Verchiel must know that I will chase him.* He doubted that the Powers leader would pass up the opportunity to take him out once and for all. It didn't look as though the angel would be alive for much longer. This had to be Verchiel's last chance to ruin it all, to stop the prophecy from becoming reality.

Aaron heard them first, the hungry crackle of heavenly fire as it cut its way through the air. He dove to the side as four daggers of flame passed harmlessly through the spot he had been hovering mere seconds before. But a fifth had been thrown in anticipation of his reaction. The fiery blade penetrated his upper thigh with a bubbling hiss, burning through his pants, plunging beneath the flesh to the very bone. It was as if someone had poured molten lava inside the wound. Aaron cried out, gripping his injured leg, attempting to stay aloft.

Then, like something out of the worst of nightmares, Verchiel dropped from the sky. The angel actually appeared to be in even worse shape, flesh in various stages of decay, wounds ripe with infection. Even as they hovered in the open night sky, Aaron could smell the nauseating scent of rot. It was as if all the evil and insanity that had shaped this once heavenly creature into what he was today was bubbling to the surface, showing the world his true face.

They fought, their powerful wings pounding

the air unmercifully. It was hard to focus above the pain in his leg, and Aaron's endurance was rapidly waning. The bitter conflict had to end soon. A sword of fire flashed in Verchiel's grasp and Aaron lashed out, kicking savagely at the angel's wrist and making him drop it, but another was already forming to take its place. Aaron kicked again, this time with his wounded leg, and explosions of jagged agony sliced through his body.

Verchiel seemed to sense the Nephilim's dwindling fortitude. Aaron could see it in his red-rimmed eyes as yet another sword of fire appeared in his hand. "You will know your better!" the angel screamed, flecks of blood flying from his mouth as he soared across the short distance of sky, sword arcing downward toward the Nephilim.

Aaron wasn't sure why he thought of it then or why he hadn't thought of it before, but the inspiration came to him suddenly, fully formed, and a weapon the likes of which he had never wielded before burst to existence in his hand. It was a gun, much larger than Lehash's pistols, the barrel long and thick. It had none of the delicate beauty of the gunslinger's twin weapons, reminding Aaron more of the guns he'd seen in some of his foster father's Friday night action movies, something that would have been used by Arnold, or maybe even Clint. Something used to take the bad guys down once and for all.

Aaron almost found the change of expression on Verchiel's twisted features comical as he raised the fearsome weapon forged from his imagination and heavenly fire. Almost. If only the whole situation hadn't been so damn sad.

He pulled the trigger, and a sound like what he would have imagined from the Big Bang erupted from the weapon. A tongue of fire at least a foot in length lapped eagerly at the air as the force of the blast tossed Verchiel back. He began to spiral down toward the church below, a tail of smoke trailing from a grievous hole in his shoulder. The once fearsome angel crashed through the large, circular, stained-glass window at the front of the Saint Athanasius Church.

Still clutching the hand-cannon forged from his imagination, Aaron followed, cautiously entering the church through the broken window ringed with jagged teeth of multicolored glass. It was dark inside, the only light thrown from the stars and the half-moon above.

As Aaron touched down upon the altar, he checked the landscape. Most of the church's religious trappings had been removed. Rows of benchlike seats were spread out before him, and a bloody trail ran up the center aisle to end with Verchiel as he crawled laboriously toward the front doors and escape. Aaron allowed his wings to catch the air and glided down the aisle, favoring his injured leg, the powerful weapon still at his side.

Verchiel sensed his presence, halting his progress and slowly rolling onto his back. The angel's breath rattled wetly in his lungs. Shards of stained glass clung to the sticky surface of his gore-covered body. Aaron gazed into the darkness of the circular wound that had been blown into his right shoulder and imagined that he was gazing into the angel's soul. It was as he suspected: nothing there but a yawning blackness.

"What are you waiting for?" Verchiel gasped through his swollen and bloody mouth. "This is your chance to destroy the one that wished with all his heart to see you wiped from existence."

Aaron raised his weapon, sighting down the barrel, taking aim at the one that had caused him so much grief. He was repulsed by this creature lying on the floor before him, the furthest thing from a being of Heaven he could possibly imagine.

Verchiel chuckled, bubbles of blood forming at the corners of his mouth. "I would have purged the world of your taint," he taunted. "Burned the ground you walked upon with heavenly fire."

But Aaron also felt something else: a certain pity for the being that had once been a soldier of God, then became so twisted and poisoned by his hatred and his inability to forgive that it had turned him into a monster.

"There would have been no one to mourn your passing," Verchiel continued, shaking his head from side to side, "for I would have slain them as well."

Aaron knew that angel was trying to goad him into action, and he decided he would not play the game. He lowered the weapon, allowing it to disintegrate in a flash.

Verchiel's face twisted in confusion. "What are you doing?" he asked, a quivering rage evident in his question. "I'm prepared to die now. Kill me."

Aaron shook his head slowly, a now familiar sensation beginning to build in the center of his chest. It was the beckoning of a higher power to release those imprisoned within cages of fragile flesh—to allow them the opportunity to stand before their Lord God and beg for absolution. It was the power that defined him as the savior of prophecy, and it coursed up from his center and down the length of his arms, emanating from his outstretched hands.

"Kill me," the angel demanded again, struggling to rise to his feet.

And though it pained him greatly, Aaron knew exactly what he was supposed to do with Verchiel. He had to let go of his anger, of his hate for the pathetic monster that had caused him and the ones he loved so much hurt. And he was better for it, experiencing the true meaning of his God-given gift.

"It's not my place to judge you," he said, his voice calm, showing not a trace of anger.

Verchiel's black, soulless eyes bulged as Aaron reached out to him. Suddenly the angel knew what was about to happen. He wasn't going to be slain by his most hated enemy.

This was a fate far more horrible than that, and he tried to flee.

Aaron reached out, taking hold of Verchiel's head in his hands, and let the power of forgiveness flow through him and into the leader of the Powers host.

"I forgive you," he whispered as the Powers commander struggled to be free of his hold. "But will *He*?"

Verchiel shrieked in fear, his sword, Bringer of Sorrow, appearing his hand. He attempted to lash out at Aaron but didn't seem able to control the fire. The sword lost its shape, the flame instead flowing down to consume his arm, eating away the wounded flesh and continuing on.

Verchiel thrashed in the Nephilim's grasp, trying with all his might to escape, but the fires of Heaven hungrily devoured his shell of flesh, leaving behind a being of muted light, one that did not shine like the others Aaron had set free. This one was different.

Aaron released the creature and stepped away from the angel in its purest form. Verchiel knelt upon the floor of the church, quivering as if cold, but Aaron suspected it was fear that brought this reaction. The frightened creature raised its head, gazing up at the ceiling, seeing far more than the images of Heaven's glory painted there.

"It was all for you," Verchiel muttered in the tongue of the messengers. The glow of his body began to intensify, and soon he was enveloped in a sphere of solid, white light, as if a star had somehow fallen from the sky to lie upon the floor of the church.

Aaron shielded his eyes with his wings, saving his sight from the searing intensity of the light. *"I am so sorry"* were the last words he heard uttered by the terrified Verchiel as he was taken in a flash.

Taken up to Heaven to face the judgement of God.

chapter sixteen

It was as if some great burden had been lifted from her.

Vilma Santiago opened her eyes in the semi-gloom of the basement room where she had been confined. She felt better than she had in days. She couldn't describe it exactly. The only thing she could even vaguely compare it to was waking up the morning after taking a really important test at school, the sense of relief she felt when she realized that the test was behind her. It was a really stupid comparison, but it was the best she could manage at the moment.

She sat up, waiting to feel the ominous stirrings of the angelic power within her, but felt nothing other than an extreme sense of calm.

The golden chains attached to the manacles upon her wrists rattled as she climbed off the mattress and padded barefoot across the concrete floor to the stairs. Slowly she climbed the steps, listening carefully, curious if there was anyone else in the house with her, but she heard nothing.

The girl stepped out into the hall and turned toward the kitchen, vaguely recalling that Lorelei and Aaron had given her something—some kind of medicine. But deep down she sensed that that was only partly responsible for the peace she was feeling.

She found Gabriel lying on the floor in the kitchen, staring out at the night through a broken screen door.

"Hey, boy," she said, happy to see the animal, strangely relieved that she hadn't been left completely alone.

Gabriel, startled by the sound of her voice, sprang to his feet, tail starting to wag when he realized that it was she. *"You scared me,"* he said as he trotted to her, nuzzling her hands for affection.

"I'm sorry," Vilma told him, stroking the soft fur of his head. The chains between the manacles jangled.

"I don't think you're supposed to be up and around," Gabriel cautioned. He leaned heavily against her, accepting her ministrations with relish. *"They told me to make sure you stayed in bed."*

"I feel better," she told him. "Much better, really." She put her arms around his neck and gave him a serious hug. "I don't know what it is, but I all of a sudden feel like everything is going to be okay."

Gabriel twisted in her grasp so that he could look into her eyes. *"Is he all right? Do you know if Aaron is safe? I was feeling something too, but I couldn't tell if it was a good feeling or a bad one."*

"I don't know," Vilma told the Labrador, looking at her reflection in his dark gaze. "I just woke up feeling that things had finally been set right." She smiled and shrugged her shoulders. "I really don't know what it means. It's just how I'm feeling."

Gabriel tilted his head quizzically. *"I guess that's a good feeling, then."*

"I guess so," she said, standing and walking toward the door. "Where are the others, Gabe?" she asked the dog as they stepped out into the cool, spring night.

The streets of Aerie were deserted. It was eerily quiet, no signs evident that this *wasn't* a neighborhood abandoned during the nineteen seventies, even though she knew otherwise.

"Lorelei said something about going to the center of town to wait." The dog gazed down toward the end of the street, nose twitching as he sniffed the air.

"To wait for what? You mean for Aaron to come back?"

Gabriel slowly nodded his blocky head. *"Or maybe for something bad to happen."* His voice sounded small, tinged with fear.

Vilma took in a deep lungful of the damp night air as she gazed up at the stars, reaffirming the peace she had felt since awakening. She wasn't sure exactly how she knew, but she was certain that something about the world had changed.

"No," she said, heading toward Aerie's center with Gabriel close at her heels. "I don't think this is bad at all."

The citizens had gathered in the center of what had once been called the Ravenschild Estates, now known to them simply as Aerie. Lehash wasn't sure exactly why they had decided to congregate not far from the twisted rubble that had once been their place of worship, but they were all here.

It was probably for the same reason that he had come, an almost palpable feeling in the air that something big was about to happen. Nobody was talking really, both fallen angel and Nephilim alike. All were standing around, gazing off into the distance or at the night sky above them. They didn't seem to know the direction from which it was going to arrive, but they knew it was coming nonetheless. He wouldn't have disagreed with them.

Legs crossed at the ankles and leaning against a broken streetlight, Lehash sucked upon the moist end of his cheroot, letting the smoke leak from his nostrils to swirl in the air about his face. He studied the gathering crowd. How their numbers had declined, thanks to the Powers' attack just weeks before. How many of them had been struck down, only to be freed from their mortal shells by the touch of the one they had come to think of as savior. *Will the rest of us be as lucky?* he wondered.

"Fancy meeting you here," called a voice from across the street, and Lehash watched as his daughter approached. She strolled down the street, careful to avoid the gaping holes that had been caused when the full fury of her angelic spells had been unleashed upon the Powers, the magick of angels igniting pockets of explosive gas trapped beneath the toxic-waste-tainted ground. She had brought a weather-beaten beach chair with her, one that had belonged to Belphegor, and she unfolded it to sit down as she reached him.

"I kind of wondered if I was the only one feeling it," she said, crossing her legs, nervously wiggling her foot as she gazed around at the center and all who had gathered there. "Guess this answers my question."

Lehash silently pulled upon the end of his foul-smelling cigar, his preternatural vision scanning the entire surroundings, as well as hundreds of miles beyond it.

"That's one thing I never could stand about you," Lorelei suddenly said from her beach chair. "You never let me get a word in edge-wise."

His daughter thought she was pretty funny.

It was a trait that she definitely shared with her mother. The gunslinger remembered the human woman he had fallen in love with, fooling himself into thinking that he could live like them. But the joke had been on him. It hadn't been one of his prouder moments, but he had left the woman, for her own good he had told himself, knowing full well that she had been with child as he headed out again alone—until he found Aerie, a place where he could belong.

"Don't know why I ever admitted to bein' your daddy," he said dryly, blowing smoke into the air to punctuate his statement.

Lorelei chuckled, grabbing hold of the long, snow white hair the hung past her shoulders. "I don't think you could've denied it," she said, shaking the hair at him. "The family resemblance is unmistakable."

Lehash removed his Stetson and ran his fingers through his own snowy hair, pushing it back on his head before replacing his hat. "Yer probably right," he drawled, the crack of a smile appearing at the corner of his mouth. "Should'a dyed my hair."

His daughter smiled, and he continued to smoke his cigar, and they waited, as did all the other citizens.

Waited for something to happen.

"What are we going to do if he fails?" Lorelei asked quietly.

Lehash looked down at her sitting in her

lounge chair beside the streetlamp as if waiting for a nighttime parade to pass by. It was a question he had been thinking since Aaron left Aerie in pursuit of his father and Verchiel. The kid was good, there was no doubting that, but the gunslinger had also seen the savagery of the Powers commander many times throughout the centuries. And if there was one thing that Lehash had become in his millennia on the earth, it was a realist.

He took a long, hard pull on his cheroot before answering. "We'll do what we've always done. We'll survive, fight if we have to," he said. "But the world's going to become a pretty inhospitable place if the boy—"

"I'm not talking about that," Lorelei said cutting him off. "I'm talking about the prophecy. What happens if he dies before fulfilling the prophecy?"

Lehash dropped the remains of his cigar to the street, crushing out the burning ember beneath the toe of his leather boot. "I guess we're out of luck," he said, feeling an icy grip of hopelessness the likes of which he hadn't felt since descending from Heaven and first setting foot upon this world.

The jangling of chains distracted them, and father and daughter both looked up to see Gabriel trotting down the damaged street beside Aaron's friend Vilma.

"I told that dog not to let her out of bed,"

Lorelei said, standing up as Vilma and Gabriel approached the center.

"I guess she felt it too," Lehash said. From what he could see, the girl seemed healthy, no signs of the furious internal battle she had been fighting earlier. The Malakim's potion appeared to have done what he had promised it would. Furtively he hoped that her struggle hadn't been for nothing.

Lehash felt it before it actually happened, as if somebody had taken a cold metal spur and rolled it down the length of his spine. And by the expression he saw upon his daughter's face, he knew that she, too, had felt it. He lifted his hands and allowed his guns of heavenly flame to take shape.

"Dad?" Lorelei questioned.

She stumbled and he let go a gun to grab her arm, keeping her from falling, all the while scanning the neighborhood and beyond, searching for any hint of trouble. Whatever it was— whatever they were feeling—was coming now, and there wasn't a damn thing any of them could do to stop it.

Gabriel began to bark crazily, his tail wagging. The dog seemed to be staring at a spot in the center of the street, across from the rubble of the church. Something was manifesting in the air there, something black and shiny, and Lehash lowered his guns knowing full well what he was seeing.

"He's back."

The gunslinger left his post and headed toward the disturbance. Lorelei followed closely at his side, and before he knew it, Scholar, Vilma, and Gabriel had joined them. Citizens from all around were converging on Aaron Corbet.

Lehash raised his hand, signaling for those around him to stop where they were, as he carefully inched his way toward the boy. He wanted to be certain that everything was all right before exposing the others to potential danger.

Aaron stood, unmoving, head bowed as if in deep reflection, his enormous wings closed about him like a black, feathered blanket. Slowly the wings unfurled to reveal that the boy had not returned alone. Two men were with him, one on either side of the young Nephilim. Lehash didn't recognize the older of the pair. He was human, with the taint of angel magick about him. But there was no mistaking the identity of the other, even with the odd addition of a mouse perched upon his shoulder.

"Hello, Lehash," he said in a voice as smooth as smoke, and the gunslinger suddenly found himself wrestling with conflicting emotions.

"Been a while, Lucifer," Lehash responded tersely, not sure whether he wanted to embrace the angel or put a bullet of fire through his head.

Aaron returned his wings to beneath the flesh of his back, a wave of exhaustion washing over him with the realization that he had made it home.

Home. He couldn't believe that he actually now considered this decrepit neighborhood built upon a toxic waste dump his home. It was kind of sad, but at the same time it filled his heart with happiness to know there was a place where he belonged.

Before he left Saint Athanasius, there had been some protest from his companions when he suggested they return to Aerie together. The human healer, Kraus, did not feel he deserved the kindness of Aerie's citizens after having served the Powers for so many years. And Lucifer Morningstar, well, he suspected that many of Aerie's fallen residents would still have issues with him.

Aaron would hear none of it. He was tired, and he wanted to return to his friends. Giving them little choice, he had wrapped his father and the healer in his winged embrace and brought them back to Aerie with him.

"Since you two already know each other," Aaron said, trying to divert the constable's attention, "allow me to introduce Kraus. He was the Powers' healer."

The old man bowed his head in reverence to the angelic gunslinger. "I am truly honored to be in your presence," he said.

Lehash moved closer, sniffing at the man. "He has the stink of Verchiel on him. The Powers commander changed him somehow."

Kraus lifted his head and gazed at the formidable angel before him. "He gave me the gift of sight," the human said, touching his face. "I was blind from birth, but now I am able to see."

"A healer, then," Lehash said, looking the man up and down. "I guess the citizens could use the help of a healer."

Lorelei moved around her father and tentatively approached Aaron. "So it's over?" she asked, as if afraid he was going to tell her otherwise.

Aaron nodded. "Verchiel's the problem of a higher power now."

A yellow streak bounded from the crowd and Aaron found himself knocked backward by the impact of his best friend. He stumbled, his injured leg barely supporting his weight, as Gabriel braced his front paws on the boy's chest and frantically, affectionately, licked his face.

"I'm glad you're back and that you're not dead," the Lab said between sloppy laps.

Aaron hugged the big yellow dog, letting his tongue wash over every inch of exposed skin on his face and neck. "I'm glad I'm not dead too, pally."

Gabriel dropped back to all fours, tail wagging wildly as Aaron continued to heap affection upon him. "How's Vilma, Gabe?" he asked. "Did you keep an eye on her for me? Is she doing any better?"

"Ask her yourself," the dog replied, looking into the crowd just beyond where he was standing.

The full meaning of the animal's words didn't quite sink in until Aaron followed Gabriel's gaze and his eyes locked immediately with hers. He practically ran toward Vilma, taking her into his arms and holding her as close as he possibly could. If he could have opened himself up and placed her safely within, he would have done so. The girl reciprocated, burying her face in his shoulder, her arms wrapped tightly around her neck.

"I knew you were all right," she whispered in his ear. "I knew you wouldn't leave me alone."

They kissed then, their lips pressing hungrily together, and Aaron finally understood what had been absent from his life thus far. He had been incomplete, a piece of him missing without him ever truly realizing it. Sure he had felt the emptiness from time to time, but he'd chalked it up to feeling sorry for himself, never knowing that there was another half out there in the world waiting to be joined with him. Vilma was that half, and at that moment, as he held the woman he loved in his arms, Aaron Corbet knew for the first time what it was to be whole.

"Is that your father, Aaron?" he heard Gabriel ask, and let go of Vilma long enough to see Lucifer moving through the crowd, talking to those who had gathered, heralding his arrival.

"Yes, it is," he said, no longer afraid to admit it.

A silence had come over the center, and only

the voice of the Morningstar could be heard.

"I'm sorry," he said to each and every one of the gathered. "I'm sorry for all that I have done, and for all that has happened because of me."

He moved among them. Whether they were fallen angel or Nephilim, all were deemed recipients of his soulful regrets. Some embraced the angel that once sat at the right hand of God, tearfully accepting his words of apology, while others snarled, turning their backs, not yet willing to forgive him his sin, or themselves their own.

Lehash, Lorelei, and Scholar were the last to receive the Morningstar's words of atonement, and Aaron wondered if he was going to have to get involved. The air became charged with tension as Lucifer approached them, and he readied himself just in case.

"Tumael," Lucifer said, bowing to the angel that Aaron had only known as Scholar.

Tumael bowed back, accepting the first of the fallen's apology graciously.

He moved on to Lorelei.

"I accept," she said before the words even had a chance to leave his mouth, and Lucifer smiled.

And then the Morningstar turned his attention to Lehash.

Aaron wasn't sure what history had passed between them, but he guessed that Lehash had at least once been a follower of the Morningstar, and the gunslinger didn't appear to be the kind of angel that easily forgave and forgot. Time seemed to have frozen as the two fallen angels stared at each other, and Aaron got the distinct impression that the two had at one time been close, maybe even friends.

"We had to be out of our minds to follow you," Lehash said, his eyes dark and intense.

Aaron watched the constable's hands, looking for the telltale spark of potential danger. The pistols were gone at the moment, but they could easily return in less than a heartbeat.

"I think we all went a bit insane," Lucifer answered, his watchful eyes never leaving the angel in front of him.

Lehash casually scratched the accumulation of stubble on his chin.

Do angels even need to shave? Aaron wondered as a bizarre afterthought, intensely watching the scene playing out before him.

"Do you think we're any better now?" the constable asked.

Lucifer thought for a moment, turning his gaze away from the gunslinger and looking at those gathered around the center of the blighted neighborhood. His mouse nuzzled the side of his face affectionately, and he reached up to gently stroke the top of the rodent's head. "I do believe we are," he answered, and he bowed his head to Aerie's keeper of the peace. "I am sorry, Lehash, for all that I have done, and for all that has happened to you because of me."

Lehash scowled as he reached inside his coat pocket. Slowly he withdrew one of his foul-smelling cheroots. "After all this time, that's the best apology you could come up with?" he asked as he placed the end of the cigar between his waiting teeth.

Lucifer stepped closer to the gunslinger and Aaron tensed, his wings ready to launch him into the air toward the two fallen angels. His father raised a hand, causing Aaron to twitch in anticipation, but he stayed where he was. The tip of one of the Morningstar's fingers began to burn white with the heat of heavenly fire, and he gently touched the tip of the cigar protruding from the gunslinger's mouth, igniting its end.

"It was kind of short notice," Lucifer said as Lehash began to puff upon the cigar. "And I never really thought I'd have this chance."

Lehash brought a hand up to his mouth, momentarily removing the cigar. "Things do have a way of working out, don't they?" he asked the angel that had led him down the path to the fall from Heaven.

"They certainly do," Lucifer responded, and the almost palpable tension that filled the air dispersed like a fast moving summer storm, the atmosphere suddenly fresh and clear.

Everyone just seemed to be milling about, basking in a strange sense of closure. Aaron knew they were all feeling the same thing. With the threat of Verchiel and his thugs removed from the equation, the citizens were now free to think about things other than their day-to-day survival—namely their forgiveness. A special freedom had been given to them this new day, and Aaron allowed himself to take a small measure of pride in the fact that he had played a large part in bringing this part of the story to a satisfying conclusion.

"It's strange," Aaron said, his arm still around Vilma, Gabriel standing loyally by his side. "This is the first time I've ever seen them happy." Even the human healer, Kraus, seemed to be fitting in, already beginning to administer to those who had not yet healed after Verchiel's attack on Aerie.

"It's nice," Gabriel said, and his tail began to wag.

Vilma gave Aaron an affectionate squeeze, resting her head upon his shoulder. "And it's all because of you," she said. "You did this. You gave them something that they'd only dreamed about."

She pulled away and studied his face. Her stare was intoxicating, and if all he did for the rest of his days was to look into those eyes, it would be a satisfying life indeed. She tapped the center of his chest with her index finger.

"You, Aaron Corbet," she said, her voice like the beginning chords of the most beautiful song he'd ever heard. "You made their dreams come true."

He couldn't have imagined a more wonderful moment, but as everything else in his life had, that too was about to change. For he was the messenger, and he had a purpose that took precedence over everything else.

Aaron felt it begin to grow deep within his chest. It was calling to him in a voice that was growing louder and stronger with each passing second.

"Aaron, what's wrong?" Vilma asked. She stepped away from him as he began to tremble.

"Nothing's wrong," he said in a voice void of any doubt. This was it; through all the battles with monsters and renegade angels, this was what it had all been leading up to. "Everything's exactly as it's supposed to be."

Aaron called forth his wings as the glow began to emanate from his hands, a store of supernatural power never fully tapped, until now. The citizens saw him—saw what was happening—and they began to smile, and some to cry tears of joy. The power that was his and his alone to wield called out, and he went to them, as they were drawn to him, seeking the absolution that had been so long in coming.

And as he walked among them, his touch forgiving them of their sins, Aaron Corbet thought of who he was and what he had become. Never would he have imagined that a foster kid from Lynn, Massachusetts, could command the power of God's forgiveness. Yet this was how it was supposed to be—how it was *always* supposed to be. Yes, there had been hardships, the loss of loved ones, and seemingly insurmountable obstacles, but from all the pain and suffering, a thing most wonderful had been achieved.

The fallen angels of Aerie glowed like gigantic fireflies, dancing in the air above him on iridescent wings that made a sound like the gentle stroking of harp strings as they flapped. Aaron turned and saw that Scholar now waited before him. The fallen angel looked anxious, gazing wistfully at Aaron and then back down the street toward his workplace.

"Don't worry," Aaron reassured him, reaching out to touch the front of his crisp white shirt. "We'll take good care of your books. I think I know just the guy to do it."

They both looked toward the man called Kraus. He had fallen to his knees, staring in awe at the constellation of angels hovering above. "I think he'll do an excellent job," Aaron said as the power surged from his fingertips into Scholar.

The fallen angel's shell of flesh, blood, and bone was burned away in an explosion of white light, and the angel Tumael was welcomed by his brethren in the air above the center.

Aaron smiled as he saw Lorelei and Lehash slowly walking toward him. The gunslinger was one of the last, and looked as though he just might burst from his skin even without the Nephilim's touch.

"This is it," Lorelei was saying as she held onto the arm of her father's coat.

Lehash kept his eyes on Aaron, saying nothing as father and daughter tentatively walked toward the constable's absolution. The other Nephilim affectionately touched him as he passed, thanking him for his protection, and wishing him well on his journey home.

The cowboy angel stopped before Aaron and respectfully removed his hat. The Nephilim raised his hand toward Lehash, the outline of his fingers barely visible within the corona of the pulsing, white power he now wielded.

"Wait," Lehash suddenly said, his own hand going up to block Aaron's touch. "I can't go," he said, and turned to look at the faces of the Nephilim that eagerly awaited his ascension. "Somebody's got to watch out for them, protect them." He looked to Aaron. "There's still so much they have to learn."

Lorelei squeezed her father's shoulder, leaning in to place a kiss upon his grizzled cheek. "We'll be fine," she said, and Aaron nodded in agreement.

Lehash took what would be his last look at the children of angel and human, and then stared into his daughter's emotion-filled eyes. "You probably will be," he said, reaching out to cup her cheek in his hand. "But there's no harm in trying to stay for just a bit longer." They both laughed, and embraced for the final time.

245

Then Lehash released his daughter and turned to Aaron, puffing out his chest. "Well, c'mon, savior boy. I ain't got all day."

Aaron smiled broadly, laying the flat of his palm against the gunslinger's chest, and watched in awe as Lehash's true form gradually took shape, the human shell shucked off like a thick layer of dirt and grime. The angel that was Lehash propelled itself skyward with a succession of powerful flaps, dipping and spinning in the air in an amazing display of aerial acrobatics, before joining the others.

"Show-off," Lorelei said, wiping tears of happiness from her eyes.

Aaron looked up at the angels of Aerie, committing each and every one of them to memory. It was an amazing sight to behold, as if the stars had come down from the sky for a closer look. He knew that he would remember and treasure this moment until his dying day, but he also knew that it was time for it to end—time for those above him to leave.

He spread wide his great wings and held his arms aloft toward them. "You're forgiven," he called out.

And one by one they left this earthly plane, returning to the place of their creation, a place long denied them, but that now took them back into its celestial embrace.

Heaven welcomed them home.

Slowly Aaron lowered his gaze from the

early morning sky and saw with a combination of shock and shame that there was one that he had forgotten.

Lucifer stood alone, a beatific smile upon his dark, handsome features as he looked to where his brethren had gone. There was a longing in his stare, but also a happiness for those who had finally completed their penance and were allowed to know the glory that was Heaven again.

"Is this for you as well?" Aaron asked, startling the first of the fallen from his meditations beyond the sky.

Lucifer held the tiny mouse in the palm of his hand, tenderly stroking its fur. "I don't know," he said sadly with a slight shake of his head. "I'm afraid to find out."

Aaron stepped toward him and gently laid his hand upon his father's chest. He felt the power at his core rise, and for a fleeting moment, believed that *it* was about to occur, that it was to come full circle, and the final forgiveness was about to be bestowed upon the one who had started it all.

But it wasn't to be.

The divine power receded deep inside him, dwindling away to but a burning ember in the center of his being.

"I'm sorry," Aaron said sadly, removing his hand from his father's chest, and the first of the fallen smiled at him. It was a sad smile, but one full of understanding and immeasurable patience.

"So am I," Lucifer said, returning his gaze to the brightening morning sky above Aerie, gently stroking the tiny animal nestled within the palm of his hand.

"So am I."

epilogue

Lucifer Morningstar stood outside the Saint Athanasius Church and Orphanage and listened for the sounds of Nephilim. There were more of them out there in the world, he knew, children of the dalliances of angels, their birthrights gradually blossoming upon their eighteenth year of life.

Happy birthday to you.

The temperature had dropped considerably in the past hour, and it had started to snow. Lucifer turned his attention to the change in weather, studying the intricacies of each individual flake as it slowly drifted down from the sky. The mouse on his shoulder curiously sniffed at the winter's rain as it fell, its tiny pink tongue darting from its mouth to lick at the water as it melted upon the jacket of the fallen angel's dark blue suit.

The summer in the northeast had been brutally warm, and it looked as though the New England winter was going to be just as extreme. But the weather did not bother the first of the fallen angels. He quite enjoyed the seasonal changes. If he hadn't, he would have suggested that the new Aerie be established in San Diego, California, instead of western Massachusetts.

The fallen angels of Aerie were gone, but the Nephilim remained. They were to be the new protectors of a world rife with paranormal dangers. Verchiel and his Powers had ignored their true purpose, choosing to focus their energies on a personal vendetta rather than the job they had been assigned to do.

As he could sense the emerging Nephilim, so could the fallen angel detect the presence of things that had no right to be upon this world, things that wished Earth and its inhabitants harm. It was now the responsibility of the Nephilim to cleanup after the Powers' irresponsibility and to keep the world of God's chosen creations safe from harm.

But there was much they needed to learn before they could take on such an enormous task, much that he, Aaron, and Lorelei would need to teach them.

They had been here for a little more than six months, the new Aerie established within the former roost of Verchiel and his ilk. The Ravenschild Estates had quite simply become too large for their lesser number. With the fallen angels gone, this was a new time for the Nephilim, a new history waiting to be forged for them as individuals, rather than victims of a genocide perpetrated by Verchiel and his host.

As for himself, Lucifer looked upon this as yet another test from his most Holy Father above. He would help to train those who would protect God's human flock, and finally, hopefully, achieve absolution for his most heinous sin.

The snow now fell harder, a whipping wind creating swirling vortexes of white that danced around the expanse of unkempt lawn in front of him. He could sense the small animals that lived in the overgrowth around the church and orphanage, hunkered deep within their burrows, primitive instincts telling them that this would be the first major storm of winter, that soon everything would be covered in a cold blanket of icy white.

And from this season of death there would be rebirth.

All Lucifer wanted was a chance to apologize to his Father, as he had to the brothers that had sworn to him their allegiance in Heaven so very long ago. But he knew that opportunity had to be earned, and would come at a heavy cost indeed.

The mouse on his shoulder whispered in his ear. It was cold and wanted to go inside. Lucifer obliged his tiny friend, taking him indoors and out of the storm. After all, there was still much to be done to prepare the Nephilim for the tasks before them.

He thought one more time of his brethren, basking again in the glorious radiance of the Almighty, and longed for the day that he, too, would be allowed to experience the Blessed Majesty once more. Was that a hint of envy he felt growing in the deep inner darkness of his psyche? Quickly he squelched it before it had a chance to take root, before it could do any harm. The first of the fallen had had more than his fill of jealousy's bitter fruit.

The price of forgiveness was indeed a costly one, but it was an amount that Lucifer Morningstar was willing to pay.

Aaron and Gabriel trudged through the quickly accumulating snow in search of the newest of Aerie's citizens.

The boy had lived with them for a day over two weeks. His name was Jeremy Fox, and he'd come from London, England. Aaron had found him living on the streets of the great, old city, begging for change and eating from Dumpsters. To the casual passerby he appeared to be just another sad example of a mental health system in desperate need of an overhaul—muttering and crying out, talking to himself as he wandered the streets of England's largest city. He hadn't been difficult to locate; the power of the

Nephilim was strong inside him, and it practically cried out to be found.

Now Aaron found the youth behind the abandoned school, in the snow-covered playground. He was sitting atop the monkey bars, sneakered feet dangling, the top of his sandy blond head and shoulders covered with collecting snow. He had not been adjusting well, and Lorelei was worried.

"Hey," Aaron said as he walked closer.

"*Hey*," Gabriel repeated, not wanting to be left out of anything.

The youth remained silent, as if attempting to tune out the strange world in which he had come to live. Aaron could sympathize; it hadn't been all that long since he was in the very same frame of mind.

It had been Lorelei who convinced the youth to listen to the story told by the two crazy Americans who seemed to appear from out of nowhere, a fantastic tale about angels having relationships with human women and the children that were born as a result. Jeremy had looked at them as if they were out of their minds, and Aaron was certain that he was trying to decide whether they were in fact real or just manifestations of the insanity that had taken hold of him since his eighteenth birthday. They had told him that they could help, and Aaron had watched a look of cautious hope fill the boy's eyes.

Taking that as a yes, not giving him a chance to refuse, the Nephilim savior had taken the troubled youth within the confines of his wings of shiny black and had transported him back to the safety of Aerie.

He had been here since, but did not seem to be adapting to his new life, clinging to his humanity, refusing to accept the reality of what he was becoming.

"Lorelei's worried about you," Aaron said, looking up at the boy sitting on the top rung of the monkey bars. "She thought I should find you—just in case you needed to talk or something."

Gabriel sniffed around the various pieces of playground equipment, his nose melting furrows in the two inches of snow that had already fallen.

The wind suddenly whipped up, causing the powdery snow to drift, making it seem that more of the white stuff had fallen in some areas than in others. The winter wind had a bite to it, but it didn't bother Aaron as it once had. *Just another perk of being Nephilim,* he thought. Hot or cold, it was all the same to them, perfectly adaptable to any climate upon the planet.

Jeremy remained unresponsive, immobile upon his metal perch.

"Guess not," Aaron said, putting his hands inside the pockets of his spring jacket. "Well, if you should need to, you know where I . . ."

The boy turned to look at him, the snow atop his head sloughing off to fall to the ground below his dangling feet. "They say that you're some kind of bloody savior," he said, his accent thick and full of repressed emotion. "What's that like, then?"

It was something Aaron tried not to think about very often. He knew that he had a job to do, a purpose and a destiny. But the moniker of savior was one that he did not wear comfortably.

Aaron came closer to the jungle gym. "Don't believe everything you hear," he said, casually taking hold of one of the horizontal pipes in both hands. "There's very little difference between me and you," he told the boy. "It wasn't too long ago that I was thinking the same thoughts you are right now."

Jeremy's features grew angry, and he let himself drop from his seat to the snow-covered ground. He came at Aaron then, chest puffed out, eyes wild. The older Nephilim held his ground.

"And *what* am I thinking?" Jeremy asked in a hiss. "Use your angel powers and tell me what's going on inside my bloody head, mate."

Gabriel had come to stand by Aaron, his nose covered in snow from his explorations beneath the cold, winter covering. *"You shouldn't talk to Aaron that way,"* the dog warned, hackles of fur rising around his neck. *"He's just trying to help."*

Aaron reached down and thumbed the dog's side in assurance. "It's okay, Gabe," he said. "Jeremy and I are just talking. He's a little upset."

The Lab grumbled something and then became distracted by a squirrel, and he bounded off in pursuit of the animal with an excited bark.

"You want me to tell you what's going on in your head?" Aaron asked the new Nephilim. "You're thinking that the world has become insane, that everything you've known, everything you've taken for granted all your life, has been flipped upside-down since your last birthday." Aaron paused. "How am I doing so far?"

Jeremy seethed with an inner rage that Aaron was all too familiar with. "You don't know anything," the boy growled, sparks of heavenly fire shooting wildly from his fingertips.

"You know how I know this?" Aaron asked. "Because I thought the exact same things when it was happening to me, when the power that was inside me—something that I didn't want or ask for—decided to take my normal life away from me." Aaron placed one of his own hands upon his chest, his gaze never leaving Jeremy's. "I thought the exact same things."

The boy's anger seemed to drain away, as if he were suddenly no longer strong enough to hold on to it. It slipped away from him, and he seemed to diminish in size, the outrage he was feeling over what his life had become seemingly all that was sustaining him.

"I don't know how much longer I can fight it," Jeremy said pathetically, the snow melting upon his face, mixing freely with the warm tears that now fell from his eyes. "I can feel it inside me—clawing to get out."

"You don't have to fight it," Aaron told him. "That's why you're here: to learn about what you truly are—to learn about your destiny."

The boy chuckled then, wiping away the moisture from his face and snuffling. "Destiny?" he asked. "Didn't know that I had one of those."

"Bet there's a lot you don't know about yourself," Aaron said. "Let us teach you."

Sometimes it wore on him.

Aaron scooped up a handful of the fresh snow and began to make a snowball. "Here it comes," he warned. The last of the snowfall had been mixed with rain, creating a slushy mix perfect for snowballs.

Across the expanse of front lawn, Gabriel crouched. "I'm ready," he growled.

Most of the time these days, Aaron felt like Gabriel at that moment, tensed, ready to confront the latest obstacle head on.

He let the snowball fly, and as it fell, Gabriel leaped up into the air to capture it in his mouth. "Good catch, boy," Aaron said, clapping his hands and praising the animal for his skills.

Gabriel proceeded to eat the snowball, crunching upon the firmly packed snow, pieces falling from the sides of his mouth as he chewed. *"Make another one,"* the Labrador urged between chews.

It was so easy to get caught up in the flow of it, to become the ultimate leader, the weight of the world upon his shoulders. He needed moments like this to remind himself that there was more to life than being the leader of the Nephilim.

Gabriel had finished his icy snack and was waiting for the next, tail wagging happily. *"C'mon, Aaron,"* the dog urged. *"Throw another one."*

He squatted down and grabbed some more of the wet white stuff. "You'll never be able to catch this one," he said in mock warning, making his best friend all the more excited.

Aaron knew that his was a great responsibility, that the protection of the world had been placed in his hands and the hands of others like him. It was up to him to make sure that they were ready for this chore, a daunting task, yes, but one that he was more than capable of performing.

"Here it comes," he warned the animal, and tossed the ball of snow as hard as he could up into the air in an arc, watching as it began its descent. Gabriel bounded across the snow in pursuit, his eyes upon the plummeting prize.

Was it the life that he would have chosen for himself? No, not a chance, but he no longer resented the fate that had been unceremoniously thrust upon him. It was his destiny, and he had learned to accept it as that.

Gabriel returned to him, snowball clutched in his mouth, and dropped it at his feet.

"What, that one didn't taste so good?" he asked the dog.

"*I'm full,*" Gabriel said, deciding to lie down in the snow and roll upon his back. Aaron laughed at his dog's antics, kicking snow onto the animal's pink exposed belly.

They both felt it in the air, a familiar disruption that foretold of a Nephilim's arrival, and recognized it as someone special.

"*She's coming,*" Gabriel said excitedly as he shot to his feet, shaking snow from his fur as Aaron scanned the open space before him for signs of her arrival.

No more than five feet away the air began to shimmer and ripple, a darker patch beginning to form at its center. Gabriel began to bark happily, tail wagging like mad. Aaron sometimes wondered who loved her more.

Vilma Santiago emerged from the ether, her downy white wings the color of freshly fallen snow parting the substance of space around her. It was amazing how far she'd advanced in such a short period of time. She, too, had come to accept her heritage, embracing the angelic nature inside her.

Gabriel could barely contain himself, galloping through the snow to see her. "*Vilma's here!*"

he said over and over again, and she knelt down to accept his excited affections. She seemed just as happy to see him.

It had been a few days since they'd last seen each other, what with getting ready to start classes at a nearby college in spring and gradually getting her aunt and uncle to accept the fact that she was going away to school. Vilma Santiago was taking control of her life, and of that Aaron was very proud.

Not long after Aerie's fallen had been forgiven, she had returned to Lynn, to her aunt and uncle. He guessed that it had been difficult, their relationship now strained by her abrupt departure from their home, but they had come to begrudgingly accept her explanation of needing some time away to find herself. Aaron chuckled with the thought. *She'd certainly done that.*

Vilma finished showering the excited Labrador with affection and proceeded toward Aaron, a sly smile upon her face. He watched as her beautiful wings receded on her back, only the slightest expression of discomfort on her features.

"I missed you," she said, leaning forward to plant a big kiss upon his lips.

He met her halfway, his own lips eagerly pressing against hers. The two embraced, and he was positive that there wasn't anything that felt better than having her in his arms. If there was, he didn't remember it.

Upon returning to Lynn, she had contacted

the superintendent of schools and had worked with him and her teachers to make up the finals and projects that she had missed with her sudden absence. In no time she had completed the necessary requirements and had received her high school diploma with honors, albeit without the pomp and circumstance of a graduation ceremony, but Vilma had what she needed to continue her dream of a college degree.

Maybe I'll complete my own high school requirements someday, he thought as he held the young woman that he loved and respected so much. But if he didn't, that would be okay as well, for he was certain that life had other things in store for him.

Gabriel attempted to squeeze his blocky head in between their embrace. *"Hi, remember me?"* the dog asked, often as ravenously hungry for affection as he was for food.

Vilma laughed, a light airy sound that Aaron had learned to adore, and bent down to hug the animal as well. "How could we ever forget you, Gabriel?" she asked in mock horror.

"I know," the Labrador responded, accepting her additional attentions. *"I am pretty special."*

"That you are, my friend," Aaron said as he took Vilma's hand in his and began to lead her toward their new home within the old orphanage.

"And how is everything here?" she asked, walking by his side through the snow.

"Fine," he answered her, "especially now

that you're here." And he gave her hand a gentle squeeze to stress how glad he was to be with her.

Vilma responded in kind with a smile that was pure magick. He doubted that Lorelei could summon anything quite as powerful.

Aaron needed moments like this, for it helped him to put it all in perspective.

"When are you two going to have babies?" Gabriel suddenly chimed in, a look of seriousness upon his canine features.

They were completely taken aback by the question, and Aaron felt a flush of embarrassment blossom upon his cheeks. Vilma fared a little better than he, covering her mouth to stifle a laugh. Gabriel did not care to be laughed at. The dog waited for his answer. She had no idea what to make of the question, but Aaron suspected that it had something to do with what the last of the Malakim had said to him before he had been taken by Verchiel.

"May I be the first to say that your children will be absolutely magnificent," the angel sorcerer had said in that strange place between worlds.

Lehash had said that the Malakim had the ability to look into the future, and had seen that he and Vilma had children—magnificent children. Aaron had never bothered to share this information, not wanting to pressure her in their relationship in any way.

"Where did that come from?" Vilma asked the dog.

"Just curious," Gabriel answered. *"I'm certain that they would be magnificent."*

Aaron felt her gaze upon him as they reached the entrance that would take them inside the building.

"And what do you think, Mr. Corbet?" she asked as he reached out to pull open the door. "Would they?"

He held the door against his back, allowing them to enter before him. Vilma waited just inside, arms crossed, as he let the door slam shut behind him.

"Well?" she chided.

"Yes," he told her, a smile upon his face that he couldn't control. When they decided to take that next step, to marry and eventually have children, he knew that it would be the most amazing thing in his life. To have a family with her was something to look forward to.

Something for the future.

"Yes, they will most certainly be magnificent," he told her.

Until then, there was still so very much that needed to be done.

As many as one in three
Americans with HIV...
DO NOT KNOW IT.

More than half of those
who will get HIV this year...
ARE UNDER 25.

HIV is preventable.
You can help fight AIDS.
Get informed. Get the facts.

www.knowhivaids.org
1-866-344-KNOW